I0598995

Spark
The Elements Book Three

Courtney Rene

Chapter One

Life is a funny thing. We are born. We live. We die. Sounds simple enough, right? But it's not. Those stages may be simple, yes. One hundred percent, yes. Those are the easy parts. It's the in between parts that are hard and seem funny to me. I am the creator of life. I can create in many forms. I can grow plants from just the idea of them. I can help to create life in animals with nothing but what can be called a small bit of energy. Easy. I can do it all without much thought.

However, creating life must come with thought. It just has to. Is it right what I can do? Is the outcome good? Is it evil? Is it wrong? Honestly, creating life is hard on the soul. Or at least it is on my soul.

Then you have the life growing inside me, that I did create, but not with any purpose or even desire. Oh, don't get me wrong, I want this life. It's wonderful and special and its mine, but it was not one I sought out and not one I actively created. In a common happenstance, it was unplanned, an accident. A wonderful, exciting, and yet scary accident.

We, being Ash, Nora, Reed, and me, have all been through so much in our short lives. We'd been created by SaneCorp through DNA experimentation. When we started showing signs of our gifts we were taken from our families, some peacefully, and some by force. We were all caged in a building where we were again experimented on. I didn't realize that was what was happening as for me it felt more like school. Until it didn't. We also hadn't known about each other. We'd each thought we were the only ones.

My gift at that time was not as developed as it is now, but I was able to grow life. That could be plants or animals. I could grow anything I wanted. Trees, roses, and my favorite, daisies. I could help animals to reproduce. Everything I touched with my spark of life energy, I could make grow, and grow fast. A tree in a day. Fruiting plants in a moment. I could also help animals reproduce and reproduce in multiples. I thought my gift and my learning was amazing.

But then, I was made to experiment on my animals I'd grown to love. Mixing creatures to create abominations. They told me I was creating new species, but all I created was pain and death. When I balked, the people of SaneCorp didn't like it. They began to punish me. Physically in some instances, but mentally as well. They would use my favorite animal friends against me. They would hurt or kill my bunnies or goats or whatever, if I didn't do what they asked. It wasn't a threat they used against me. It was a promise. Do this now, or Reggie will die. My heart couldn't take it.

One night, after Reggie, my sweet mini white and black goat I'd created and raised from a baby, had been taken and murdered in front of my eyes, for not doing as the scientist had demanded, I decided I couldn't do it anymore. That night, after the building went quiet, I opened a window and grew myself an escape route, in the form of a tree. It was a mix of several types, but mainly oak and willow. I wanted something strong enough to hold my weight, and I wanted it to grow fast. When it reached my high window on the fourth floor, I climbed out with only a bag that held a change of clothing, and I ran. I had no money. I had no idea of the world outside that building. I just ran.

We, again meaning me, Nora, Reed, and my Ash, we'd all had about the same reaction to being at SaneCorp as children. We reached a point where escaped was the only option, and we scattered out into the world. I ended up at a small farm in New Mexico and made a life until Reed found me. The others arrived in my life not long after. We'd taken on Dr. Dane, who'd gone mad trying to give himself what we had.

We'd then tried to work with SaneCorp, thinking a home was better than a life on the run, but that didn't work either. We found out they were trying to make us into weapons they could use against the world. We also found they were still experimenting on people, and not in a good way. Death and destruction followed. We'd had to take on Creed to escape. To do that, we'd burned the place to the ground. Well, Ash burned the place down.

We left that burning building, and were again on the run, with no idea where to go or what to do. This time though, we had each other. And we knew we were stronger as a group. We would be okay if we stayed and worked together.

Looking at the faces staring at me, all with many different states of emotion on them, I knew they were feeling some of what I was too. A baby was wonderful, beautiful, and yet it was not a good time for it. Maybe that is why it was such a miracle. It happened when I and Ash were actively trying not to have a baby.

However, maybe blurting out that I was having a baby had not been the right course of action. Especially considering all that was going on.

"How long have you known?" Nora asked from where she was turned around in the front seat of the car, so she could look at me. Her shoulder length hair once colored black and purple, was now the bright white of her natural color she'd tried to hide. She'd kept touches of the purple here and there for, as I liked to think flare, but maybe because she knew the people of SaneCorp had disliked it. Either way, it suited her.

I decided to be honest with them. Reed, Nora, and especially Ash deserved the truth. "I thought maybe I was a few weeks ago, but I didn't want to know. So, I pretended to myself it wasn't there. I know now that I have known for a while. Even if I didn't want to see it or feel it, the energy had been there, and I knew about it from the moment it sparked to life."

"Eve, why didn't you say anything?" Ash asked from where he sat next to me in the back seat. He took up a lot of space in that back seat. His warmth emanated from where his body touched mine, making me feel soft and safe even if the discussion was hard. We were parked in the berm of the road in front of a growing field of soybeans. We had just left the SaneCorp building where, as we were making our escape, I'd sprung the reality on the other three. Reed in the driver's seat had turned with a jerk to look at me with his dark piercing black eyes wide in shock, after I'd voiced the simple phrase of "Oh, by the way, I'm pregnant."

The car had swerved sharply before he'd gotten it back under control. He'd quickly pulled over to the side of the road, where we now sat on a small road surrounded by fields on one side and a thin forest on the other. I looked out over the field of beans and felt the concern, fear, maybe a bit of anger at the situation from the other occupants of the car. Not at me. I knew it wasn't at me. It was there though, a bright red emotion swirling about us, all the same.

Nora sat, calmly turned in her seat and looked at me where I sat in the back seat behind Reed. She was studying me, but not upset really. One way to tell with Nora was the car was not cold and there were no little snowflakes floating about. Those were always a dead giveaway when she was feeling anything heavy.

They were all waiting for my answer to Ash's question. "I was afraid. Not of any of you, but to say it out loud. It would have made it real. I was afraid of what would happen if the company knew. If anyone found out. We know they were listening to everything we said and watching everything we did."

We sat in silence for a few moments. I was deep in my own mind wondering what to do and where to go from here. They probably were too. I was proven correct when Reed asked, "Well, what's our next move? We can't sit here all night."

"I think we should get as far away from here as we can," Ash said while looking at me.

Nora nodded her agreement, but Reed looked at me from the rear-view mirror and seemed to be waiting to see what I would say. He was good like that. Watching. Thinking. A load of patience, while I worked it out.

"I think we should stay here," I said.

"What!" Ash said. Or yelled, depending on how you wanted to look at it. He was obviously not expecting my response.

"Why?" Nora asked. She, however, was still just a calm force within the mix of many emotions.

Reed again stayed quiet. He was giving me a chance to say and explain my reasons.

I spoke carefully, but with a firm purpose so they would know I had given my answer some thought. It was not just a whim. "We have been running for a long time. Each of us in our own way. I thought we could stay at the compound here and be happy. We could be together and safe and not running and fighting for our lives anymore," I said.

"Eve, we can't stay at the compound. We just set it on fire," Ash said as if I didn't remember.

"No, we can't stay there. But we can't leave either. First, we need to stop running. We need to fight for ourselves and our lives and now I need

4

to fight for this child. I am not going to allow this baby to live and know only a life of running and fear. I don't want them to always be looking over their shoulder. You felt that way once too. You sought us all out to end the running. I'm ready to make that happen. This ends here for me. You guys can do what you think is best for you. I'm not the boss of anyone, but I'm staying."

"Eve," Ash said and took hold of my hand. My hand felt small in his. I could feel the callouses on his palm, rough against my own. I could sense the strength and energy he held within himself. He was so gentle with me, yet he was raw strength inside. The energy that raced around in him was immense and heavy.

"Plus, I have this desperate need to know what the company was doing here. We have an idea, but we don't know. There were hundreds of people on the list of missing. Where are they? And did any of them survive whatever SaneCorp was doing to them? Are there others like us out in the world? What happened? Don't you guys want to know?"

Nora and Reed shared a look. All Reed did was lift and drop one shoulder. Nora gave him a tight smile then turned back to me. In that moment I knew they were on board. They didn't seem to need to talk to each other to communicate sometimes, but I was able to read them better than they probably expected.

Nora and Reed weren't mind readers. That was not one of their gifts. They communicated with their eyes and their body language. They knew each other so well they just seemed to know what the other was thinking.

I turned to Ash and asked, "What are you thinking?" He sat there, my hands in his and his bright amber, red eyes on mine. His face pale in the low light of the car. His hair black as night had grown in the last year. It was long and straight down to his shoulders, but that day as he'd done more often than not, he'd tied it up in a ponytail bun at the crown of his head to get it out of his way.

"I am thinking I understand what you're saying. I hear you. Part of me even agrees with you, but I don't want you anywhere near SaneCorp. I don't want them to know about you or the baby or anything. I can't do it Eve. I can't put you and our child at risk. You understand what I'm saying, right?"

"We have to do this, Ash. You know it. We can figure it out. I mean look at us. We have powers that are awesome and together we are badass," I said.

Nora and Reed both laughed. The sound thankfully broke some of the tension that felt heavy in the confines of the car.

"Cussing doesn't sound right coming from me, does it?" I asked with a rueful grin.

Ash squeezed my hand. "No, babe. Not at all."

"I'm going to win this argument. It's my turn," I said to the car as a whole, but to Ash specifically.

I watched several emotions cross over Ash's face before he looked to Nora who nodded once. He then turned to Reed, and they stared at each other for a moment, quietly communicating in a manner I didn't understand. I saw Reed lift one dark eyebrow. Was that the answer? It must have been as Ash turned back to me, and said, "Okay, we need a plan. Then we will see."

Chapter Two

We drove into the little town where we had been unexpectedly putting down roots the last few months. We stopped into the pizza shop, where the big and loud owner smiled at us and asked, "Large? Half cheese, half meat lovers?" He was a big and robust man. He had dark hair, dark olive skin, and dark chocolate-colored eyes. He had a smile of genuine welcome that I loved. His energy felt soft and clean. He was a good person, which was all I needed to know.

He also likely ate a lot of his own food, and it showed in the size of his girth. He liked his food to be good, and that showed too in the fact the pizza was a favorite of all town people. The shop was always clean and tidy, so you knew he took pride in his restaurant.

I always took note of all these things when I entered this place. Actually, when I entered any place. I may seem small and fragile, but I'm not. I knew where the exits were. I knew where all the people were within the building. I knew what I could potentially use as a weapon. I felt the energy all around me and knew what areas of weakness there were. I could create life, and that was a gift all in and of itself. I was figuring out though that creating life was not my only gift.

Reed stepped up to the counter, paid for the order, and we all found a quiet booth toward the back in a dark corner. We planned our future there, while we waited for our pizza to cook.

"We can run over to the community board and see if there are any for rent postings," Nora said.

"That's a great idea! We can also stop in at the library and use the computers to see if we can find anything online too," Ash added. Not surprising. He was more tech than tactical in many ways.

"We will need a yard or some land so I can grow a garden. We can set up at the market during the week and help bring in funds," I added. It was more than to just bring in funds. The market was a way to stay connected to the people. The goings on around town.

"Yeah," Ash said, "and I can go over to the computer repair shop over on the corner by that one deli place and see if they need any help. Something part time so we have time to do some mystery solving and preparing."

"I'm pretty good as a waitress. I have loads of experience," Nora said. She looked over at the counter and then said, "Actually, be right back." We all watched her as she got up and went to the counter by the register. The owner popped out of the back, and they talked for a minute. They both nodded in agreement and then shook hands.

"I got a job. Four days a week," she said after she scooted back into her spot.

I think we were all a little shocked for a moment, but Reed stepped in with his sarcasm that we all had come to enjoy, "that was fast."

Nora just shrugged and said, "Didn't see any point in waiting. We will need cash and fast. I will make minimum wage plus tips, so it's a good deal."

Reed smiled and kissed her head. "No time like the present, I guess. I can help Eve at the market hauling and dealing with customers as I did before. I will also see what other types of job I can find around here. I'll pull my weight just like everyone else.

"Of course, you will," I said. "None of us thought otherwise."

"Wasn't worried, bro," Ash chimed in.

Our pizza arrived and we spent the next few minutes eating and, in my case, and I suspected the others too in our own heads contemplating our next steps and the future.

I think we all felt a little concerned, even if none of us said it. We had all our needs met over the last few months. All our food and housing, our clothes and makeup had been provided for us. There we were sitting in a pizza place, on the outside looking calm and fine, but we didn't even know where we would sleep that night.

As we cleaned up our table, I asked a question I'd never thought I would need to know. "So, I know this is a little intrusive, but how much money do we all have? I have a bank account with about Thirty grand in it, but it's not easy to access as the bank was a local bank out west. I can get to it, but it will take me setting up an account here and transferring everything."

"I'm not destitute either," Nora said. "I've got a little over forty-five grand or so. Thankfully, it's in a national bank so I can get to it easy."

"Me too," Ash said. He turned to the table and with a giant cheeky smile said, "I've got plenty of money. Close to a hundred grand."

I'm sure my eyes were as wide as saucers as I heard the amount. "Where did you get all of it!"

He laughed and looked at Reed when he said, "I'm sure Reed is about the same as me. I didn't always live by the rules in my past lives. The world was screwing me, so I took what I wanted."

"Oh my God," I said under my breath.

Reed laughed as well. "I don't usually want to be lumped in with other people but yeah, Ash is right. I'm pretty well stacked with..." He looked at Nora and me for a second, and Ash for a long moment then said with a huge sneaky smile, "close to two hundred."

"Thousand!" I gasped.

"Show off," Ash said softly. I heard him as I was next to him, but I think the others did as well as both Nora and Reed laughed.

"Yeah, thousand," Reed said.

"But where did all the money come from?" I asked with I'm sure they thought of as prudish judgement, but it wasn't. Not really. It was genuine awe. I thought I was doing good with about thirty grand saved up and here they all were with a lot more than me. Even Nora had half as much more than me.

Ash looked at the table as a whole and then directly at me and asked, "You swear you won't get mad?"

"Can't promise, but I don't think I will," I said.

"Well, I don't know about Reed, but I'm a bit of a hacker as you all know, so I just did a bit of hacking into SaneCorp's financials and took what I deemed they owned me."

Reed chimed in, "Well I apparently deemed they owed me more than you did, as that is exactly what I did too. Just took a bit from each account at first. Then I set up a direct deposit like I was an employee."

"Seriously," Nora said.

He shrugged and then said, "I get a paycheck from them every other Friday."

"How do you know they don't realize it's you?" I asked.

He just shrugged again and said, "So, what if they do? I move the money from the account as soon as it deposits every other week. I have several accounts with several different institutions. I pull cash when I need it. Haven't needed it since being here, but once I do, I'll drive out of town for a bit and then withdraw what will last us a while. Next time we need it I'll go to a different location and do the same."

"Aren't you worried they will find you or us?" Nora asked. She indicated me with a tilt of her head.

"We aren't going to be hiding," I said. "Not really." Before Ash or either Nora or Reed could say anything to that announcement, I continued, "I mean, once we decided to stay here and become detectives, we knew we are not going to be in hiding."

"But the baby?" Ash said.

"Which we will be hiding," I said emphatically. "As much and for as long as possible. Once I start showing, I won't come into town. Or I won't come into town around people."

The others just stared at me. "I don't want to run and hide forever. I know none of us do. Not really."

"But we need to keep you and the baby safe," Ash said.

"I understand what you are feeling. I understand the need to keep us safe, but Ash, I'm not a hot house flower. I know I look sweet and innocent and weak, but I'm not."

"I never said you were," he said.

"None of us did, Eve," Nora said.

I held up a hand to stop them and said, "I know you never said that, but you all treat me like I am anyway. I'm not mad about it. Everyone my whole life, outside of my parents, have always seen me as this small, sweet, ethereal creature to protect. I promise, I will pull my weight."

"I never thought otherwise," Reed said.

"Dude," Ash said and flipped him off.

Reed just laughed. "You guys forget we spent several months together. She's a tough cookie."

Nora shook her head, but she was smiling. Ash shook his head too, but he was not doing so in humor. He was annoyed. Maybe a bit jealous, which should have annoyed me too, but instead it just made me want to hug the angst right out of him. So, I wrapped my arms around one of his bigger ones and said, "Don't get jelly about a few months in the past. You and me, and Reed and Nora, are right where we were meant to be."

He squeezed me back and placed a kiss on my head. "I know. I can't seem to help it," he said.

"No worries, man. I think we all have the same problem. I think it was built inside of us to be a little proprietary over our partners," Reed said.

Nora nodded with a rueful grin and said, "Yeah…I'm the same way. I don't want to be, and I try to force it back, but it's there all the same."

I thought about it and agreed. "I'm in the same boat. I love Nora, but there are times, she is just too smart, strong, and beautiful."

Nora laughed. A sound which burst out of her in a pop of joy. "Oh, you are too funny. Me? Beautiful, strong, and smart? Girl you just summed up yourself too. We are a pair. Green over the other, even when we shouldn't be."

"Okay," I said. Then turned to Ash and said, "So, we know where and how Reed keeps his money, what about you? Are you as sneaky with yours?"

He lifted one shoulder and said, "Nah. I'm not much into cloak and dagger stuff. I just put it in a bank outside the US. One they don't have the right to demand information and access too."

That made sense too. "I'm not techie smart like you guys, but I'm thinking maybe I should learn to be."

"On to the next issue," Nora said. "Where are we going to live?"

"Let's go over to the notice board and see what they have listed for rent there. If we can't find something there or at the library, we can always ask around at the Farmer's Market," Reed said. "Those people are the helpful type."

I lifted an eyebrow and said, "Those people?"

"Yeah, the family oriented, environmentalist, self-sufficient types. If there is anything I have learned after all the time spent at farmer's markets with you, it's simply they love being helpful."

"Come on then, before it gets too dark," Ash said.

We all cleared our table. Nora said goodbye to the owner saying she'd be in the next day to see what schedule he had for her. Then we headed out and walked over to the hardware store where the community board was.

The walk over was lovely. It was still early days but felt like full summer. The air was hot and sticky, but there was also a warm breeze that helped to dry the sticky from your skin. The sun was just starting to set, and the day was beginning to cool. Thankfully, it wasn't so hot that Nora would get sick, but it was hot enough that I was basking in it.

The store was about two blocks away and it was a nice walk. My hand in Ash's bigger one. There wasn't much conversation going around between us, but it was a companionable type of quiet as we enjoyed what was left of the day.

Once we got to the board there were several options. "What about this one?" Nora said. Then she looked at it closer and said, "Oh never mind."

It was an apartment, with two bedrooms, but no backyard or yard area at all as it was in town and backed up to a parking lot.

There was another apartment, but it was also in town. It said it had a small outdoor area, but it didn't sound like a usable area. More like a sit a chair in the space type of area.

"This looks good," Ash said. It was an advertisement for a doublewide trailer outside of town. It sat on one and a half acres, of which would be the responsibility of the renters. It was a bit heavy on the price but with the four of us, and what I now understood to be a heavy savings, we would be okay.

We called the number on the flyer and a man named Randy answered. We set up a time to meet him out at the place the next day and that was that.

"Looks like we are hoteling it tonight," Nora said.

"Do we want the trucker's inn or the chain?" Reed asked.

"I say the inn," Ash said. "We can get separate rooms on the ground floor in case we need to bolt, but still have a bit of privacy."

"Sold," Reed said. We walked over to the inn, got our rooms, and we said our goodnights. Nora and Reed in one room and me and Ash in another.

After checking the room for bugs, and locking the door securely, Ash flopped on the bed and said, "It's been a day. I'm not sure I'm going to stay awake for long."

He was not wrong. We'd had a rough one. Setting a building on fire and running for our lives would do that to you. I lay down next to him on the bed, tossed a leg over his body and said, "So? What do you think?"

He didn't pretend to not understand me. "I'm happy and I'm scared at the same time."

"Do you think it's a mistake?"

"No. Timing is a little rough, but never a mistake. We will figure it out and keep our little nugget safe and sound. We will be the parents we never had. I think it will be a little hard and a lot scary, but we got this. Plus, we have Nora and Reed, and you know they will be right here with us and the baby. They aren't going anywhere. Especially right now."

"I don't know what to do or how to prepare. Should I get a doctor? What if the baby is…different?"

Ash sat up and took my hands. "Then all the better. But if you are worried about the baby starting fires in the crib or growing trees in their room, I am not sure you need to. We didn't get our gifts until we were older. Four and five years old for all of us. I think the baby will come out looking just as normal as any other baby. We will just need to watch them as they grow. If they get gifts, then we will deal with them. If they don't, then we will deal with that too."

"You have it all figured out, I see," I said while giving him a squeeze.

"I'm sure we will be figuring it out for the rest of our lives. This is just one more bump in the road to learn and get over. This is a good one though. This is a wonderful surprise gift we get to be a part of. I'm excited. Aren't you?"

"I am. But like you, I'm also scared. I think that is why I tried to pretend it wasn't there." I sat up and then crawled over Ash to sit on his stomach so I could face him as he lay on the bed. "Ash, I admit I knew the moment there was that spark of life inside me. I felt it. I knew, but I tried to pretend I didn't. I tried to talk myself out of being pregnant. I was scared about what you would do or say. I was scared about what the company could try to do to them. I am so scared of all those things now too, but I want this baby."

I put my hand over my nonexistent baby bump and said, "I can feel it in there, growing and living. It's like a warm hum. Just under my skin I can feel it."

Ash sat up and wrapped me in his arms. "I can't feel it. Not yet, but I will. We are going to be awesome parents."

Chapter Three

The next few days went by in a flash. We met with Randy to discuss the rental of the trailer. It had three bedrooms, a living room, one bathroom, a small laundry room, and a relatively updated kitchen. It had a dish washer and everything. The land was about an acre, full of tall weeds, and new trees trying to grow.

"Can we clear the yard and put in a garden?" I asked straight away. It would be a deal breaker if he said no.

He looked over the weed and debris covered lawn and said, "Do what you like. Don't think much will grow for you though."

We all smiled, knowing it would grow just fine for us, or me in particular.

"When can we move in?" Reed asked.

"Do the furnishings stay, or will they be removed?" Nora cut in.

Randy gave us each a long look then said, "Move in can be as soon as you pay the deposit and first month's rent. Furnishing, keep what you like, burn the rest."

That was a little disconcerting. Ash must have felt the same and he said, "Burn them?"

Randy turned to face Ash directly and said, "Yeah, don't want any of it."

There was a story there, but I wasn't brave enough to ask what it was. Apparently neither was anyone else as Reed just pulled out a wad of cash from his pocket, counted out enough funds for the deposit and the first month rent, and said, "I guess we got a deal then. We will move in today."

"Got any pets?" Randy asked.

Everyone looked at me, which I couldn't be upset about. I gave a small laugh and said, "Not yet. Will that be an issue?"

"Naw, just keep 'em locked up. Animals tend to go missing out here," he said.

Well, that was ominous. I wanted to know missing as in taken or missing as in dead. "Okay. Thanks for the warning," I said knowing I wouldn't get answers on either one.

"Yup." Then, "I put the number for the water and electric people on the table. Don't got no gas. Heat is all electric. It can get expensive so watch out for the bills and pay it on time. They won't mess about with you and will turn them off without notice."

"Thank you," Reed said and reached out to shake Randy's hand. "We will pay on time. You won't have to worry about that."

He stared us all down for a second more. He looked like he wanted to ask a question, but as we had before with him and the furniture, he apparently decided against it. "Let me know if you have any problems out here."

"Will do," Ash said and shook his hand as well.

Randy stepped into his shiny black truck and settled down in the seat. Before he closed the door he said, "Good luck!" Then he slammed closed the door, started the car, and drove off in the direction of town.

"Good luck?" Nora asked in the suddenly quiet yard.

I felt suddenly giddy with excitement. I did a little jig and spun around the yard. I could feel everyone's eyes on me, but I didn't care. I took a deep breath in of the fresh air, the dirt, and the grass and said, "You smell that? That's freedom." Then I laughed and spun around again. "And it's ours!"

Ash gave a shake of his head, but there was a giant smile on his lips. "Let's see what all the place needs and get to the store. I have a feeling shopping may take a while."

As we had not left with much from the compound, we would certainly need some personal items. There was also not a scrap of food in the house, which was to be expected. As for the furniture, the place was well set. The kitchen was stocked with plates, pots, pans, and utensils. Anything else, we could get as we needed it.

"I want clean sheets though," I said as a must have.

"Agreed," said Nora. "I'm good with hand-me-down stuff for the most part, but sheets and underwear are a no thanks."

"Which is why I just go commando," Reed said.

I couldn't help but laugh at him. It wasn't the words he said, but how he said them, that made it so funny. He said it so bereft of emotion it was like he was talking about bread. However, I saw the little sparkle of humor in his eyes. Nora must have too as she laughed right along with me.

"Really, dude? They don't need or want to hear about your underwear situation," she said.

"How do you know? They might be dying to have that information," Reed replied again just as deadpan as before.

"Ew, bro. Just no," Ash said with a look of pinched disgust.

"We will need a few seed starters too. Things that are local. It's easier or quicker I guess, to start plants made to grow in the area. Plus, if people see us getting seeds and such, they tend to think less about how often we are producing."

"Lord, more tilling," Reed said with an exaggerated eye roll.

I shook my head and said, "No, out here it won't matter if it's tilled or not. We can just cut down the weeds, put down a layer of weed blocker paper, add a layer of dirt and mulch and I can get to it.

"That's definitely easier than tilling," Ash said and he and Reed high fived as if they were getting away with something.

"You guys will still need to mow and keep the yard tidy. I'll take care of the garden and stuff, but the rest of this outside work is up to you guys."

"Sexist much," Ash said.

He was kidding and we all knew it, so I replied with, "Yep."

After the lists were made, we went into town. They guys dropped Nora and me off at the big box grocery and marketplace store to get that type of stuff, while they went to the hardware store to get a few parts to fix up the mower they found in the shed, as well as get me the seeds, mulch, and stuff I needed. I did not leave it up to them to pick my seeds on their own. I made them a list just for that.

By the time we made it back to the trailer, had everything put away, it was the end of a very long, but also productive day.

We'd had dinner, which consisted of homemade soup and fresh bread bought at the bakery in the grocery. We'd all cleaned up and put away what we could. I was setting up Ash's and my bed by putting on the freshly washed sheets and blankets. Suddenly, I felt an unsettling in the air. I lifted my head and tilted it to try to hear better through the thin trailer walls.

"Do you hear that," I whispered to Ash who was finishing putting away the few clothes we had, in the one dresser in the room.

His head flew up to look in my direction. "No. What do you hear?"

"I don't know," I whispered. "It's just something off. I think it's an animal." I pushed out with all my senses and tried to connect to it. All I was getting was red.

"Oh! It's hurt," I said with dawning realization. I dropped the blanket I'd had in my hand in a pile on the bed and rushed to the door to the trailer.

Ash held the door tightly closed just as I reached it. "Wait," he said. "We don't know what's out there."

"I do," I said firmly. "It's one of my wolves. He's hurt. He is looking for me to help. He knows I will.

"Eve," he said. Just one word. I could feel his worry. How could I not. Even if I hadn't been able to feel it, I could see it bright and clear on his face.

"What's going on?" Nora said from the doorway to her and Reed's room.

"There's an injured animal out there. He needs help," I said.

Reed popped his head around the door frame over Nora's and said, "You going out there? Alone?"

"No, she's not," Ash stated.

"I'm going out there. With or without you, but I'm going. Make up your mind what you're going to do as I'm walking out the door in two seconds. One..."

"Fine, we can all go," Ash said while staring down Reed and Nora as if challenging them to deny him.

"Sure, let's see what's going on," Reed said.

"Yep, let's go," Nora agreed.

Ash stepped back and I swung open the door and quickly stepped outside. Ash jumped out the door and tried to get in front of me at the same time. "Dude. The animals are my forte. Move," I said and with my arm pushed him aside.

He let me move him out from in front of me. We all knew it, but no one said anything about it.

"I just want to make sure you're safe," he grumbled.

I sighed and tried to gather my patience. I walked with firm purpose toward the shed at the back corner of the property. I reached for my center, where I could always find a wealth of energy. With my mind, I pulled it forward and sent out waves of warmth and feelings of safety in the direction of where I felt the pain. I was still new with this animal communication thing, but I knew this animal was a wolf. It felt like it was one I'd reached out to before at SaneCorp. It felt familiar and I didn't feel afraid.

I came to the front edge of the shed and squatted down. Ash hovered menacingly over top of me. I sighed again, but he was getting on my nerves. My patience was one of my virtues, but it was not a strong one lately. "Ash, back off a little."

"I'm just trying to make sure the animal doesn't attack," he said.

I stood up and turned to face him eye to eye. "I said…back off."

There was something in my tone I'd not heard before and from the wide eyes of not only Ash, but Reed and Nora as well, it was not a tone they'd heard from me either. I didn't have time to baby him though. The wolf was hurt and reaching out for help. They could either help me or get out of my way.

Ash raised his hands in a placating motion and took a step back. I took that as a sign he was finally listening to me. I bent back down and mentally called out to the animal. It took a moment. One filled with deep silence, but finally, I could hear heavy paws on the ground and the long grass singing with the slide of movement against the blades. Then out of the darkness, two glassy eyes appeared at my face level, followed by a long thin body, of the expected wolf.

There was pain and fear coming off it in waves. I stood up and walked closer and then placed my hand flat on its head. He didn't shy away or flinch. He stood stoic and calm before me. Once my hands connected with him, I was not afraid at all. The same cannot be said for the others. I could feel their fear coming off them in a rush of dark blue, the same as I could feel the red pain and fear coming off the wolf.

"If you guys could step back a bit more. You're scaring him," I whispered just loud enough for them to hear me.

They all took a step back but even so, I heard Reed say, "We're scaring him? I'm about to crap my pants over here."

"Seriously, dude," Nora said a bite of annoyance in her tone.

"I'm being serious. Do you see the size of that animal?"

I did. Yes, he was big. At least a hundred and fifty pounds of strength in the form of sleek muscles. It was dark, but I could see enough of his coat to see there were shades of white, grey, and brown fur covering his big body. He had a mask of black on his face and socks of black on each of his feet. He was big and he was gorgeous.

With my hand on his head, I could get a sense of his entire body and it was then I realized what was wrong. The fire, at the compound, had spread and consumed the fields around the building. It had chased the animals into the forest, but they had not been strong enough or fast enough to outrun it entirely. Some had fallen behind. Some had perished. While still others were burned. The pain was thick in the scorch marks on his feet and underbelly. But there was also pain at the loss of several members of his pack.

I looked deeper into his thoughts and pushed a bit more of my energy toward him as I tried to see where the physical pain was coming from. I could sense the pads on his paws were raw. Every step was an agony. I felt an aching burn on his undercarriage. It was painful on the inside of his back legs, and along his chest under his front legs, just the tip of his tail was singed. Finally, there were a few scorched areas on his side and back.

I don't know what made me do it. It was all instinct at that point. I wanted his pain to stop. I wanted to be able to help him. So, I did. I reached toward what I can only describe as the energy in the air, in the earth, in the plants, and even in the wolf himself, and I pushed a spark of it toward the pain and the hurt.

I use energy to create and to grow living things, it made sense I should be able to use it to heal too. That is exactly what happened. In what felt like only a moment, I sensed the pain fading and even better, the skin was healing. I felt the hair take root and push new growth where it had been lost. I felt the edges of the open burns begin to pull in and the burn shrink and then fade away entirely. What was even better, I was able to feel the wolf's relief. He didn't understand why or how the pain was gone. He only knew it had, and I had something to do with it.

When I didn't feel anymore aches or need, and the red waves were no longer emanating from him, I took a deep breath and began to pull back. It was as I began to disconnect from the wolf that the world tipped on its axis, and I felt my head spin out of control.

I sensed the wolf quickly move away from me and back into the safety of the darkness. I barely saw or heard him go as my head was whirling.

"Eve!" I heard Ash shout. Then I heard quick footsteps racing in my direction.

Before I could even sit down on the ground to gather myself, I was in his arms. "I'm good. I just need a moment."

"What were you doing?" he asked.

"You were still as stone for a long time," Nora said from where she'd squatted down next to me. "We were getting really nervous, especially when you didn't respond when we called to you."

"I'm sorry," I said, not exactly sure what I was apologizing for other than from the tone of their voices alone, I could tell they were upset. I had not meant for that to happen.

"Seriously, Eve. What were you doing?" Ash asked again.

Before I could respond Reed squatted down in front of my face and looked directly and firmly into my eyes with his dark black ones. "You were standing there, for a long time."

"Forty-two minutes!" Ash interrupted.

"Are you okay? We called to you and both you and the wolf, neither of you even blinked an eye," he continued.

I'm sure my eyes were wide open at that. Forty-two minutes? I had stood there communicating with a wolf for forty-two minutes! Well, I'd done more than just communicate with it.

"I'm sorry," I said again. "I'm okay now. Let's all just sit down a moment. I need to tell you what just happened. What I just did." I was excited about the new element of my powers. This was a game changer, even for me.

Nora promptly sat down and pulled Reed down next to her. "Sit. Let's let her rest a second. She looks like I feel when I use too much of my gift."

Reed and Ash both sat down too. Reed next to Nora, and Ash behind me as a sort of human chair. "Is that what happened," Ash asked. "Did you overuse your gift?"

"I didn't know that could happen with your gift," Reed said. "Has it ever done it before?"

"I didn't know either, but I think Nora is right," I said. "I think that is exactly what happened."

They all were just looking at me. Waiting for me to tell them. "I healed the wolf," I blurted out.

Silence greeted my words. Then they all started to talk at once.

"What? How is that possible," Reed asked.

"How do you know, "Nora asked.

"Can you do that?" Ash asked.

"I felt it happen as I did it, so I guess it is possible and something I can do," I said. "If you think about it, it makes perfect sense. I use my gift with the energy around me to grow things. I just used it to grow new hair and grow new skin. I took away the pain as the body healed. That was all I was trying to do when I started out. Stop the pain. Then I felt the healing and I knew that was exactly what I was supposed to be doing. My gift is more than just lemons on a tree or double egg yolk eggs from chickens. It's a real gift of healing. Why did I never think of healing before?"

"Eve, that is amazing," Nora said with a genuine aw in her voice and expression.

"I agree," Ash said with just as much amazement.

"No," Reed said, "This is dangerous."

"What? Why," I asked.

Ash turned to Reed and although he didn't say anything we all could see the same questions on his face.

"Because," Reed said, "they already knew about her gift of creating. They've chased us all over the country our entire lives for what they knew we could do. What do you think they will do when they find out she is not only able to create, but she can heal too? Oh, and by the way she's also growing a human baby made up of two elements. No, this is really dangerous."

Reed was many things, and gentle was not always one of them. He was blunt and honest to a point. But he was also not wrong either. "Okay, so what do you think we can do about it?"

"I don't know, but we need to be aware of the consequence of it," Reed said.

"I agree, but I also want to be in amazement over what I can do too!" I snapped. "At least for one single moment."

"Well, yeah," Reed started to say, but I cut him off.

"No, I get to be happy about this. We all have these beautiful gifts and we all can do these amazing things, and I finally have one with real use and substance and you just poo poo it down."

"I wasn't," he said and put his hands up as if to calm a horse, which further incensed me.

"Yes, you were," I said. My tone was not quite yelling, but it was one small step away from it.

"Eve," Ash said in his own calming voice.

I whipped my head around and stared him down, "Don't you, Eve me! I'm not wrong. I get to be amazing once in a while, instead of a cursed creature that is evil and made from hell as an abomination!" Okay, I was now yelling.

"She's not wrong," Nora said.

With that single sentence from Nora, my anger poured out of me. I felt myself deflate at her immediate agreement with me. Then I realized I'd just attacked two of my dearest friends. One my partner and lover and the father of my unborn child. I dropped my head as a wave of shame washed over me. "I'm sorry," I said to them all. "I don't know what came over me. I was just suddenly so angry. It's not an emotion I'm used to."

"You have nothing to be sorry for," Nora said. "I meant it. You are not wrong. We should cheer and celebrate our little wins, our gifts, and what we can do and what we continue to learn we can do. We are amazing! We cannot let our fear of what might or could happen or who might or could find out, scare us into a dark life of nothing but fear and hiding."

Nora suddenly stood up and clapped and shouted out into the night. "Eve, this is amazing! You are amazing. You can heal and create. I am genuinely proud of you."

I felt my face burn with both shame at yelling at everyone and with pride at the same time because Nora was right, I was amazed in this. "Thanks, Nora. And even though I meant every word I said, I feel like I should apologize to you guys for how I said it. So, I'm sorry."

Ash gave me a quick, but tight squeeze and said, "I'm sorry too. Honestly, I was getting more and more scared the longer you just stood there, like a statue, locked eyes with the animal. I've seen you do some incredible things and I've seen you use your gifts so many times, but this was different, and it scared me."

"I agree with Ash, I'm sorry too for how I reacted. Nora is right. You are amazing, Eve," Reed said.

That was why I loved this group. Even when I was mad and slinging angry words at them, they still listened to the meaning behind them and heard me. They didn't hold my emotions against me and any anger or hurt quickly faded between us. I felt my eyes start to burn and tears begin to form. "You guys are the best!"

Reed a bit on the dramatic side for once, rolled his eyes so exaggeratedly his head rolled as well and he said, "She's crying. Ash, she's crying. Make her stop!"

"Aw honey," Nora said and started to chuckle at me. "Don't cry."

Ash seemed to take Reed's sarcasm and run with it and said, "That's it, who do I have to fight? Which one made you cry."

I laughed through my blurry eyes and unshed tears and said, "You guys. I'm so happy to have you all. Thank you for finding me and staying with me, even as I'm a complete emotional mess." I don't know where all the emotion was coming from, but I suddenly wanted to wail. I didn't though. I took a deep breath, pushed down some of the overflow of feelings and smiled at the group. "Thanks guys. I really do love you all."

"Hey," Ash said.

I turned my head to give him a quick kiss on his smiling mouth and said, "You more than anyone."

He gave me a private soft smile back and said, "Ditto. You are my world. Don't you ever forget it either."

"Okay, enough sap. Anyone want to talk about the little pack of wolves who are heading our direction?" Reed asked.

"I was aware of them coming, but I didn't want to scare them away, so I was waiting until they were ready to come into the light. Which, I think is now," I said.

Ash pulled me tighter into his arms. I had an idea he didn't even know he was doing it. "What do they want from us?"

"Not us," I said. "Me."

"Okay, what do they want from you," Ash asked.

Reed had stood up and stepped in front of Nora. She shoved him aside and stepped beside him while looking up at him with a very telling expression. Reed just shrugged and said, "Can't help it."

"They want me to help them." Before any of the group could ask any more questions, I continued, "Some are hurt, some are scared, some are just part of the group and came along because they are part of the group. Yeah, they need me to help them."

"No," Ash said. "It took a lot out of you to heal just the one!"

"I know, but…" I started but Ash cut me off.

"No. No buts. You can't do it again. Especially with the baby."

"Don't use the baby against me, any of you." I turned and looked at each of them individually before I continued, "I know myself. I also now understand what it takes to heal. I will be careful, and I will need you all to stay close and call me out if I need help."

"Eve, I really don't like it," Ash said.

Reed stared hard at the ground for a moment then said, "I don't know that it's something we get a say in."

"Thanks," Ash said with a heavy weight of thick and dark sarcasm.

"No, you gotta look at it from her point of view," Reed said. "She has a need and a calling to use her gift and to heal. That's why it is presenting now. The pack is probably screaming at her to help them. I don't think she can turn them down. We all know Eve, and we all know it's not in her make up to leave and not try to help."

"How do you know what she needs!" Ash asked. The words were normal words, but the tone was not.

Nora stepped in and said, "Because we aren't as close to it as you are. You are right in the emotion of worrying about Eve. You can't step back and see the reality. That's how Reed gets with me, and it's annoying as hell!"

Reed shrugged again, which was his usual response to many situations.

"You all know how much I hate it. He knows it and he can't stop being that way and I can't stop using my gift. I think this is another one of those pairing things. We worry about our person and in some ways to our detriment."

Ash closed his eyes and took a deep long breath. Then he said, "Okay. I'm not leaving your side though."

What I found the funniest about the situation was they weren't worried about the wolves attacking me. Oh no, they were worried about me wearing myself out. I found that extremely humorous. Of all the things my gifts had given me, this one came with a bit of humor.

I stood up. Ash mirrored my movements and stayed at my side. He was so close to me that I could feel the heat from his body. I walked back toward the shadows next to the shed where the little group had gathered. I took stock of the group and what I was facing. Some were hurt pretty badly. Not as bad as the big male I'd already healed and calmed, but still they were in a great deal of pain. Some were just burned in small areas, and some were unhurt physically, but their minds were chaos and full of fear and panic.

"I don't know which ones to help first," I said.

"Just go one at a time," Nora said.

"I get that," I said. "I mean, do I help the easy ones first so I can get them out of the way quickly, or do I help the ones that are going to be harder to heal and take more time first, so they get relief."

Reed, Nora, and Ash looked at each other, but as no one said anything, I guessed they didn't know either.

"I think I will start with the easy heals first. That way I can get several done quickly. Give relief to as many as I can the fastest. Then I will take a break and work on the harder ones. I feel like there are only two that are going to take a lot of time. The rest should not be too long or intensive."

I stepped forward to begin and felt Ash brush up against my back. "Babe," I said and turned to face him. "You have to give me some space. Why don't you go sit with the others. That way if I need any help, you are close enough to offer it, but not so close that you are…in the way."

He gave me a stern look as if to say, "be careful", and then he did as I asked and went over to sit with the others. I was then able to turn around and face the little pack of hurt wolves.

I sat down on the ground with my legs crossed over each other and regarded them all. I reached my energy out toward the little female closest to the front and mentally put the suggestion of asking her to come over to me. She was small but I could tell she was strong. Her chest, even covered in the thick multicolored fur, looked muscular, which made her appear more than capable.

She made to move toward me, but it was not without hesitation. She took a few steps and then stopped. I felt her fear of me. I felt her fear of the unknown. I felt her anger at the fire, and I felt her pain. I reached out to her mind and sent her feelings of warmth and caring. I tried to convey my desire to stop the pain and heal her. I tried to convey I, or we, were safe to her and her family. Healing the body was not all that hard. Yes, it was new, and it was taxing, but it was just a matter of pushing healing energy. The mind, in animal form at least, as that's all I'd managed to work with so far, was hard. It was more than just willing it to heal. They had to let you inside to see and feel. It was almost as if I was taking the mental pain into myself and shuffling it off from there. But to do that, she had to let me in, and she had to trust me to keep her safe.

She came toward me a bit further but again hesitated a moment before coming to stand almost nose to nose with me. I tried not to be nervous, but it was not easy. Especially with her warm and moist breath wafting over my face and down my neck. She was so close the force of her breath was pushing my hair out to wave about as if in the wind. I sensed she was trying to be big and strong and scary, but as I could read what she was actually feeling inside, which was hurt and fear and even sadness, it didn't work on me. Not entirely anyway.

I continued to press feelings of warmth and kindness and safety toward her. When I felt she was as agreeable as I could get her, I reached out my hands and very gently placed them on the sides of her face against her long snout. I felt the warmth of her body and the soft but bristly white and grey fur that lined the front of her head. The rest of her had longer fur in mostly white and grey, but there were darker browns and blacks weaved in here and there giving her a very striking, individual look.

I pushed into her mind how beautiful she was. I sensed her confusion at my compliment. Beauty is a more human attribute, I suppose. I realized she didn't understand beauty in the way I was using it. She would understand an attractive attribute like strength, but not the human standard of beauty. She was beautiful though. I moved away from beauty and instead focused on her being good. I figured she would understand good. She knew the fire was bad. She knew hunters were bad. She knew food was good. I figured she could understand being good. So, with that focus in our minds, I reached out and worked on healing her. I pushed the sparks of energy in through her cheeks where my hands rested and led them through her body toward the areas she registered as painful.

I healed as I went, starting at the angry burn on her neck that singed the fur completely off and left the skin black, red, and oozing. I pressed the healing energy from within myself and from her body as well, mixing her natural healing properties with my gifts to speed the process up to a point of watching the skin turn from the gooey mess to soft fresh pink and black skin. The fur began as little pinpoints of color before they burst forth to cover the once broken and painful patch with a new shiny crop of hair as good as, if not better, than it once was.

I then moved forward through her body and completed the process at each and every place I found pain. I found a few of the pads on her feet burned terribly. How she was able to walk, let alone stand on them was amazing. Her underbelly was raw and blistered. Her tail had several areas that lacked fur and were harsh with open wounds.

As I made my way to the end of her tail, I mentally turned back around to do another sweep of her body to make sure she was perfect. It was as I checked her belly again that I noticed something else. Something wonderful. A new member of the pack was on its way. I smiled and sent joy to the wolf. I tried to share with her I was also carrying a new member of our own special pack. I don't know if it was real, but it felt like she understood. It seemed like we had a moment of shared understanding and bonding. Yes, I was healing both her body and mind, but what we shared through our impending motherhood was special outside of that bonding. This was a gift between us. I looked into her dark brown eyes and slowly moved forward to lay my forehead on hers and we just took a moment to breathe. It was her secret as mine was. The pack would figure it out sooner or later. My pack already knew.

When I felt her start to pull away, I moved back as well, to give her space and dropped my hands from her head. It was then I realized I was tired. Healing bodies was a big deal physically. But the mind connection and the healing of the mental stability was exhausting. How was I going to get through all of them?

I gave myself a mental shake and decided I would get through them one at a time. I would have to get through it. They would be healed as fast as I could. It might not be as quick as we would all like, but they would get done. One way or another.

The little female seemed to realize as well how many still needed attention as she turned away and trotted back over to rejoin her pack. She did turn back and give me a look, which I took to be a thanks, whether it was or not. At least with that look, I knew I was making a difference.

I picked an easier one next. A young male who only had some mild burns. Nothing too damaging either body or soul. I could get the next one done quickly and move on to the next, while I recovered my mental strength, so to speak.

I don't know how long it took exactly, or how many breaks I had to take to either get a snack or a drink, but I healed the rest of the pack that night. By the last one I was totally done in. The wolves could see it and I know my friends could see it.

After the final wolf made its way back to the safely of the group, Ash came over, and lifted me into his arms and said, "bedtime for you." I didn't have any strength even if I'd wanted to, to argue the point. I was just as ready to hit the hay as he was.

"They are going to stay with us," I said.

"Who is?" Reed asked from just behind Ash's shoulders. He and Nora stayed close as well. Safety in numbers works for wolves and people.

"The wolves. They think they owe it to us to watch out for me," I said.

Silence was the response I got. "You don't mind, do you?" I asked.

"No," Ash said. "We don't mind. I'd guess we are all just thinking about what that means."

"I guess it means I have more protectors," I said.

"It would seem so," Nora said. Then the three of them laughed. I didn't understand why. I figured the more protection we had, the better!

Chapter Four

I swear Ash had just set me down on our bed and then the sun was up and shining in my face. I wanted to just roll over and go back to sleep, but this was a new day and a new start. I jumped up out of the bed and hurried to get dressed. I had only managed a shirt when my stomach lurched. I stood up and went completely still. After a moment, I felt okay again. I reached for a pair of jeans and as I leaned over, my insides did a crazy weave and heave. I threw the pants as I turned and flew out the door of my room and raced to the bathroom where I slammed open the door, and immediately threw up the entire contents of my guts in the toilet.

Reed popped his wet head out from the side of the shower curtain where he had been busy showering off for the day. "Dude!"

I dropped down to the floor and laid my head on my forearm where it rested on the toilet seat. "Sorry. It just hit me. Couldn't wait." I reached over and flushed the contents away but stayed where I was to get my bearings.

"Nora!" Reed yelled.

After only a few seconds I heard Nora enter the already small bathroom where there were now three people housed. She obviously took in this situation and found it incredibly funny as she laughed. Like a loon. I didn't find it funny as I was still really queasy.

Reed obviously didn't either as I'd interrupted his shower by forcing him to listen to me retch three feet from him.

"I'm sorry," I said again. I would have quickly exited the room but the movement of me trying to get up caused my tummy to whirl again and I found myself with my head back in the toilet heaving. Thankfully or maybe not, there was nothing left in my stomach, so it was just me dry heaving in my undies and a t-shirt, with Reed naked and grumbling in the shower. Nora found the situation completely humorous and couldn't stop laughing.

"What is going on?" Ash said as he squeezed into the already overly crowded room. "Oh honey," he said and squatted down next to me. "Stop you guys, I don't think Eve finds this funny."

Nora continued to chuckle as she answered, "I'm sure she doesn't, but I do. Look at Reed's face!"

I followed Ash's look toward Reed and if it was any other time but now, I probably would have found the humor in it too. Reed was so disgusted while trying not to appear so, his black eyes were huge and wide. The wet hair he has started to grow back was black as night, slicked back against his head, which made his eyes look all the bigger against the expanse of his pale forehead. All I could see of him was his head, neck, and a diagonal of skin across his torso, as he was clutching the shower curtain tightly in two fists against his chest like a little scared child.

He noticed us all staring at him and instantly stood up taller and quite indignantly said, "If you are all done in here, I'd like to finish my shower without a crowd and without someone tossing their chunks right next to me."

Nora hooted all the louder, but she stooped down to help me up. Her on one side, Ash on the other. I slowly, so slowly, stood up and waited to see if my stomach was done rebelling. It still felt yucky, and my muscles in my abs were sore, and my throat burned, but I think it was done trying to make me puke.

As I shuffled my way out of the room I turned back to Reed and said, "Really am sorry."

As stone faced as you could imagine, he said not one word. He just gave a little upward nod of his head, then snapped back the curtain for a bit of privacy. "Close the damn door!" He shouted out behind him as we exited. I heard the quiet click of the knob and figured Nora had given the man the privacy he deserved.

"Well, that was a great way to start the day," I said trying to lighten the mood. Nora released my arm after she confirmed I was steady, but she stayed next to me all the same.

Ash didn't let go or loosen his grip on me at all until I was back in my own bed, all tucked in as if I'd never left.

"I bet," Nora said.

"I'll grab you some water. Don't move," Ash decreed and pointed a finger at me as if I didn't know he was talking to me. Since I didn't feel like moving, I didn't argue or give him any flack for ordering me about.

Nora gave me the once over and asked, "You sure you're good?"

"Yeah," I replied as I closed my eyes. The sun was suddenly too bright. "Just surprised me is all. I had no control over it. It hit and that was that. Whatever was inside my tummy was coming out!"

Nora giggled. I must have made a face as she immediately sounded contrite when she said, "I'm sorry. I just keep seeing Reed's face. He was mortified."

As she was right, I smiled a small smile, and said, "Maybe he should shower at night for a while."

About an hour later, I got up a second time. After Ash had babied me for a bit until I got annoyed and sent him away, I had laid in bed and taken stock of myself. I don't normally get sick at all. Maybe it was part of my healing gift, I just healed myself before I even realized I was ill but throwing up was a first for me. Did not particularly like it either. After I checked myself out and felt around internally to see if it was going to happen again, I slowly, tried again.

My pants were on the floor where I'd thrown them. I bent down but did not bend over and picked them up. Then, again without bending over, slipped each leg in and pulled them up. So far so good. I slid on a pair of flip-flops and made my way to the kitchen. I didn't feel sick anymore, I was very happy to note. In fact, surprisingly, I was starving.

I headed through the silent and empty house to the kitchen where I made oatmeal with honey and had a can of lemon line soda. I figured the fizz might keep my stomach quiet.

With only a passing thought about where the others were, I decided to go outside and see where the best place would be to set up our garden. I needed to get it started if it was going to produce enough to sell at the farmer's market.

I kicked off my flip flops and stepped outside. My bare feet hit the sun warmed grass, and I gave a small sigh of contentment. I headed out to look at the property and survey what I thought would work. As I walked, I sent out what I was starting to think of as mental feelers to see where the pack was. They were currently off to the north of the property in a small, wooded area keeping cool in the warmth of the day. They seemed to be doing okay from what I could tell. No pain or fear that I could sense. Yep, all was good with them.

I wondered if my invasion into their minds or bodies felt intrusive to them. I know when Dr. Dane had tried that with us and then Creed did it with the boys, it felt wrong and downright evil. I hoped the animals didn't feel that way with me. I wasn't coming from the side of evil. I was coming from the idea of helping and safety.

As I walked, I thought about our powers. Our gifts could go either way when it came right down to what was good and what was evil. I could use my gifts to harm, but instead I used them to grow food and beautiful things. I used them to heal not hurt. Nora could do harm with her ice and snow. Reed could take the breath right out of people. Ash could destroy and use his fire to decimate anything. We all had used our gifts in harsh ways over the course of our lives, but it was not because we were bad people. It was because we were in bad situations. Situations we were put into due to others that we had no choice or control over.

We were people, and we had the capacity to do evil, but we were good people who were striving to be the best versions of ourselves. That made all the difference. I knew if Dr. Dane had even a smidgeon of any of our powers, he would have used them for power or money. I didn't even have to think about Creed. He was trying to get powers of his own for his own evil purposes. He'd almost made it to that point too. Had we not stopped him, I have no doubt he would have.

I realized had we not stopped him when we did, he could have been more than just dangerous. He could have become a monster. We were lucky we got to him when we did and took him out.

I stopped in my tracks and put my hands on my hips to survey the spot before me. As my feet were bare, I could feel the earth under my toes, and it felt fertile. It felt ready. The area was overgrown and had bare spots here and there from lack of care, but it was the perfect spot otherwise. There was a big oak tree not too far away that had long wide branches full of leaves. It would have loads of nuts come the fall, but for now, it would provide shade in the late afternoon, giving my soon to be garden a needed break from the beating harsh rays of the summer sun. Yes, that was the spot.

Now where was everyone? "Ash!" I yelled as loud as I could.

I didn't get any answer. Seriously, where did everyone go? I tracked back to the house and toward the front where the little gravel driveway was. The car was still there. "Hello!" I yelled.

Nora and Reed came around from across the road and Ash soon followed. "Where were you guys?" I asked as they got into speaking distance.

Reed slung his arm around Nora's shoulders and pulled her in close to his side. "Nora said she felt a pond over there, so we went to check it out."

"Oh," I said. Then, "Wait. She felt the water?"

"Yea, she said she could feel it in the air," Ash said. He came over to me and gave me a quick kiss. "You feeling better?"

I grabbed him at the elbows and pulled him in towards me again. I gave him more than a quick peck on his mouth. I wanted to feel the warmth of his soft lips against mine. I wanted to feel the life energy that coursed through his body. I wanted to feel his blood race and his heartbeat in a fierce rhythm. As I drew away from him, I knew I'd done exactly that. His body was humming with energy. "Yes. I'm feeling much better."

"Get a room!" Reed said.

I gave Reed an innocent smile and said, "No worries. We have one." Then I turned more toward Nora and said, "I didn't know you could feel the water in the air? Is that new?"

She gave a half answer and said, "sorta." Then she elaborated, "I have always felt it around me, but it was never that far away. Like I knew where puddles were without looking. Or I knew if a place had a water leak. I don't just feel it. I smell it and maybe even taste it in the air."

"Ooh that's cool," I said.

"I've never sensed a body of water that far away before though. Usually, it's just something close by or under my feet. The pond I sensed. It was far." She turned to face Reed and asked, "How far away you think it was?"

"I'd say about a mile. It took us a good half an hour to get there as we had to trudge through fields and forest to find it. My Nora is more than just a gorgeous face. She's pretty awesome."

She was. We all knew it too. I wasn't always sure she knew it though.

"So," I said and turned to face the group as a whole. Then I gave them a big bright smile and said, "I think we need to start the garden."

Reed threw his head back and said "Again?"

Ash wasn't much more thrilled than Reed, but he didn't exaggerate his, "Didn't we just do that?"

"Look you guys know we need to get a garden sorted so we can get set up at the market. The market does more than just bring in money. It sets us up to build relationships with the town people. We can get information from them while getting to know them," I said. I wasn't upset with their unexcited emotions about getting me a new garden set up. We had just done one at the warehouse before we burned it down. Their reaction was fair. I didn't like it, but it was fair.

"Ugh," Reed said. Then he and Ash both seemed to look at each other at the same time and decide to give me what I wanted. "Fine. Where do you want it?"

I wasn't worried about Nora. I knew she would help. "I have the perfect spot picked out around back. Come on, I'll show you!"

Nora linked her arm with mine and quietly asked, "You sure you're feeling up to this?"

I nodded. "I'm good. Much better than this morning, for sure."

"Okay. Let's get on with it then," she said and allowed me to lead the way, with her at my side and the boys following behind.

"I figure if we just burn the spot and get rid of the weeds and growth, I can make the rest work without much work. You guys know what to do."

Ash asked me to lay out exactly where I wanted it to go. I walked the boundaries I had set up in my mind with all of them and explained my rationale for it with the oak tree.

Ash stepped forward and asked Reed, "I'm going to go in vertical lines. You got the control wind ready?"

"I'm on it. Go when you're ready."

Ash jumped around and shook his arms and hands like he was getting ready for a fight. "What are you doing?" I asked.

"Making you smile," he replied.

"Babe…garden," I said and pointed to the ground.

He gave me a big smile and said, "Stand back."

He gave a little snap of his fingers and fire burst forward. It was bright with orange and red waves of color. It dropped down in an arc to the ground and caught the dried grasses and weeds in their flames immediately. Black smoke started to rise into the air as the fire grew and spread in the confines of the area I had marked out.

Ash was controlling the fire. Reed was controlling the air or in reality the oxygen, and not letting the fire go where we didn't want it. They may not have realized it or even want to admit it, but they worked well together. I side eye looked at Nora who looked back and me and we communicated without words, we both saw it. I smiled. She gave a one shouldered shrug but smiled back all the same.

The air was starting to smell a little on the smokey side. I took a deep breath of it in, as I liked the smell of burning. Not the burning of trash or plastic but of earthy things such as grass or wood, those smells I found made me happy.

I closed my eyes and reached out with senses to the world around me and caught a slight unsettling off to the north. I snapped my eyes open and focused in on my wolves. The scent of fire in the air was not making them calm and happy. It was setting them off into fear and in some of the ones that had been more seriously hurt yesterday, it brought terror.

Nora took hold of my arm to get my attention and asked, "What is it?"

"The wolves. They don't like fire. It's upsetting them."

Nora looked at the boys as they burned my garden patch to prepare it for planting. Then she followed the plums of black and grey smoke as they lifted off the ground, swirled around in the air before blowing away. "What do you want to do?"

"I don't know right off. I'm going to try to reach out to them and calm them down. Let them see it is not an out-of-control monster out to hurt them as they seem to see it as being." I took a deep breath. Slowly let it out as I focused all my energy on my small pack of frightened wolves. I sent out calming vibes and feelings of safety. In effect saying *it's okay, it's okay. You are safe.*

I focused a big dose of my attention on the big male. If I could get him to see we were safe, he would be able to make the others see it as well. I tried to show him in his mind what we were doing, but he didn't understand. So instead, I tried to tell him Ash was good. Ash was safe. He was making the ground good. How to explain you are using a dangerous thing to do a good thing? Finally, I just kept pushing vibes of calm and safety at him. He was listening or thinking about it at least.

It was like I could see them, even though they were far away. More I could see them through their own eyes. The smaller newer members of the pack were focused on the leader. The leader was watching the others to see if there would be a problem. I was getting all that information at once and trying to get them to hear me.

I gave a quick glance to see the progress of the fire clearing and was thrilled to see they were almost done. Just a small bit left to do. I continued to push calming thoughts and energy at the others and then began to add in it was almost finished. No harm done. They were safe.

Ash extinguished his flames, turned, and dusted off his hands as if he'd been doing more than just directing the flames and said "There you go. Done!"

"That was a lot easier than digging, that's for sure," Reed added as he pulled the air away from the flames on the ground and extinguished them as well.

I don't know how Reed's gift worked. He never shared anything about it. If you watched him though, he didn't seem to be doing anything other than looking. Like just then, he hadn't been active at all. He was only looking at the flames and then they were gone. One of these days, I wanted to ask him how his gift worked.

"The wolves are upset," Nora told them. "Eve's trying to calm them down."

"They are holding their own actually," I said. I'd sent them the news the fire was out, and they were now in the clear. The big male, in a manner that seemed so simple, let the others in the group know all was safe by simply…laying down. Once they saw him calm and settled at ease, they followed suit and did the same. The small moment of potential crisis was over.

"I think they are good to go," I said. Then I looked at my new area of freshly burned soil and was giddy. "Thanks for the garden spot! I love it."

"What do you think the wolves would have done without you?" Reed asked.

I shrugged and said, "Likely they would have just run. But as they are closer to town now, that could have brought other dangers with it. A pack of wolves running amuck around people is very different from them running crazy though fields and forests. That was my fear. They would just take off and head right toward people. They have been through a lot, thanks to us. I wanted to save them from that at least."

I checked on the wolves once more and found them enjoying the day quietly lazing about again. Good. They were set for now. "So, we need to go into town. Who wants to go?"

"Me!" Nora said and raised her hand as if back in school. "What do we need from town?"

"Me too," Reed said. "Where my woman goes, I'm there too." I was certain Nora was trying very hard not to roll her eyes. Reed said things like that just to get a rise out of her. We all knew it. He knew we all knew it too. I think that was why he did it. To annoy all of us in one shot.

"I'm in," Ash added.

"I want to go back to the garden center."

Ash raised an eyebrow at me. They'd gotten me seeds the day before in the town run. They also knew I could make whatever I wanted to grow, grow, so I understood the confusion. "I need to make sure we are growing things that are local. I can't bring out a case of pineapple and be like, hey I grew these myself. People would ask questions. I want variety, and varieties for this zone. We can mix it up next year, but for now, we need standard things. Now that I have my garden, I want more than I thought I did yesterday, when I did my list. I want to see what the garden center has already started and available."

"Okay, give me about ten minutes and I'll be ready." Nora said.

~ * ~

Back in town, we did another grocery run for things we'd forgotten yesterday, and I got several plants I could get started on along with the seed packets we already had. Then we stopped at the farmers market, and got sorted with getting our spot back, starting the next week.

While we were there, we stopped by a few of the stalls to say hello to some of the people we knew or faces we recognized. I say we, but I really meant me. The others just smiled and followed along.

"You guys could at least say hello, smile, or something," I grumped. Heck, they didn't even seem friendly half the time. They stared at the people and made them all nervous.

"You know who we are. This is us. We don't smile."

That came from Nora which annoyed me. "Yes, you do. I see you smile all the time with us."

"That's different. I like you guys," she said and punctuated it with a smile.

"What is your excuse?" I turned on Ash.

"I am looking out for everyone. Checking people out. Making sure we are all secure and safe. Your job is to schmooze the people. Mine is to keep you safe."

"Ash is right," Reed said. "Everyone is scared of me, so why bother smiling at them?"

"Maybe they wouldn't be scared of you if you smiled," I said.

Nora snorted.

I sighed. I knew it was a losing battle, but geez. A little help would not hurt. "Whatever."

As we were driving back home, I thought it had been a productive day all in all. Garden was ready for me. We had groceries. We set up registration for the market. Yep. Not a bad day. We could now focus on the real reason we'd stayed. To find out what SaneCorp was doing and had done to the people in that town.

We'd gathered a lot of data before leaving the SaneCorp compound. We had the missing persons list. We had the list from SaneCorp of subjects. We also had a list from the journalist of the people found in the forest. We could use them to determine who was still MIA and needed finding. Dead or alive.

"Do you think we could use the wolves to scour the forests for more dead body piles?" I asked out of the blue in the quiet car. You could tell it was not a question they were expecting as even though the interior of the car had already been quiet it had been a calm quiet. With my question, the energy in the car became heavy, instantly.

Ash gave my hand a squeeze to draw my attention to him fully and said, "I think that is a you question. You know them better than any of us do. You would know if it were something not only that you could ask them, and they would be willing to do. Also, you would know if they would understand what we are looking for."

"I think they could help us," I said. Then I laughed and said, "I just need to figure out how to explain to them what I want them to do. Not sure how to do that yet. I'll figure it out, though."

Nora turned around from the passenger seat up front and said, "If any of us could figure it out, it would have to be you. You are not only the green lady that has abilities with plants, but you are also turning into the beast master too!"

"I saw that movie, once," Reed interjected.

"What movie?" Ash asked, which I was happy about as I had no idea what movie Reed was talking about either.

"The one with the big dude who could control all the animals," Reed said. Then, "It's old. From like the 80s maybe."

"We'll take your word for it," Nora said after surveying our facial expressions and seeing they matched her own confusion.

"You guys have no movie culture at all. It's a real shame," Reed said while slowly shaking his head in disbelief.

Later that night, Ash and I were lying in bed. He was tucked up behind me with his arms resting around my ribs. I was in that place where I was not quite asleep, but not awake either. Sorta dozing and relaxing. I was warm and content. I knew Ash was still awake though.

He proved me right when he said, "You don't talk about the baby very much."

I wasn't expecting that statement, but he was right. I didn't. "Does that bother you?"

"I don't know. Maybe a little," he answered. "I guess I don't understand why."

I sat silent for a moment and tried to gather my thoughts, but he spoke again before I could respond. "Do you not want it?"

"It is not that at all!" I answered firmly and turned within his arms to face him. The room was dark but for the pale moonlight that came in through the uncovered window. His face was one that usually looked harsh and extreme to many, but not to me. I loved the harsh lines of his cheeks. The sharp brightness of his amber, red eyes. His lips were full and may appear hard and firm but, were in reality, warm and soft when against mine. His hair had grown in since we'd first met. Where it had once been shaved at the side and long on the top and back, now the sides were also growing in, and it was harder for him to pull it all back away from his face in a ponytail. So, the top was still tied back usually, but the sides he had started to tuck behind his ears. It was a great look on him. I loved running my fingers through all that thick, soft hair.

"I do want it. I'm just…afraid of hurting it," I finally answered him while looking deep into his eyes as I confessed my fear.

"Why would you think you could hurt it? Ever. Eve, you are the gentlest and most giving out of all of us," he asked.

"You know what I used to do when I was little. All the animals I hurt. You know what I did."

"Eve, you were a child. That was not on you. I know it haunts you, but you have to let it go. We all did things we aren't proud of. We are better people for it now."

"I know that in my head. I get it. But my heart says otherwise. I may have been a child, but I knew something was not right with it. Even then. All the horrors I created. All the death I caused with those animals. It's hard to just let go of," I said.

"Okay, but what does that have to do with our baby?"

"If I don't talk about it, then I don't think about it. If I don't think about it, I won't have the need to reach out to try to connect with it. I don't want anything to happen to it. I want it to have a normal growing pattern and birth," I tried to explain.

"Eve," Ash tried to interrupt but I continued right over him.

"I don't want to accidentally push my energy into it and have her grow too fast or multiply or whatever. I don't want anything but a natural, normal pregnancy for it."

"I hear you. I agree with you too. I want the normal for our little nugget," Ash said.

That little term of endearment in the form of a nugget did get a smile out of me. "So, I am trying very hard to just…leave it alone."

"What would happen if you connected to it?"

I shrugged and said, "I don't actually know. I could connect with it and feel it and know it, which would be so nice. But I could also cause her to grow quickly and be born early. Let's face it the longer she stays inside me, the longer she is safe. The moment she emerges, she's in danger of being stolen, found out, hurt, and any number of things."

"You are a protector, Eve. Why do you think you would not be able to protect our child, especially while she is still safe and cradled inside you?"

"But what if I can't control my gifts in a bad way? For just one moment, what if I harm it?"

Ash stayed silent a moment, so I reached out to see what he was feeling. I wasn't trying to read his mind. I didn't want to be invasive like that even if I could do it. I just wanted to see what he was feeling. What emotion was heaviest. I was surprised to see it was just love.

"I know you, Eve. We were made for each other. I want you to listen to me and have faith in me like I have in you when I tell you, you would never hurt our child. Intentional or not. You would not do it."

"But," I said and then I was instantly cut off this time.

"No buts. Trust in me and trust in yourself. This baby, this child of us, will be strong and perfect and wonderful. We will make sure of it."

I laid there in the darkness a long time. I laid there quietly in Ash's arms after his breathing evened out in sleep. I laid there while the moon made its slow journey across the night sky, and I came to terms with what he said. I decided to trust in myself as I trusted in Ash. With the decision firmly made, I gently reached out to the tiny little life inside me and just said, "Hello."

There was a very small stirring within my mind as my child, connected back with me. The life was too small and unformed to be able to really send anything back other than a knowing of who I was and a warmth I took to be our first tie, binding us together.

I placed my open palm on my still flat tummy and allowed myself to sleep—really sleep for the first time in weeks.

Chapter Five

Morning came and with it, another round of horrendous morning sickness. Thankfully, no one was in the bathroom this time when I went streaking in there. Ash was still in bed when it hit. I'd tried to slide out of the bed without waking him, but it was like the moment I got vertical, my stomach rebelled.

He came in after me and honestly, I know he was trying to help, but that was not the time to ask me questions. "Get out!" I shouted at him when he said, how can I help? After the wave was over, and I'd cleaned up a bit, I went to find him.

He was sitting at the kitchen table drinking a soda. I crawled onto his lap and laid my head on his shoulder. "Sorry."

He wrapped his arms around me, rubbed his chin on my head and said, "No worries."

"Still. I have never shouted at you like that before. I feel bad," I said.

"Well," Nora said as she plopped down at one of the other seats at the table, "maybe don't try to make a vomiting person give you directions. Then you won't get yelled at."

I buried my face in Ash's chest. It maybe wasn't nice, but Nora was spot on. I tried not to laugh.

Ash knew it anyway. "Ha ha," he said without any inflection. "I was yanked out of a dead sleep to find her tossing her guts. I plead my confusion on not being fully awake." He ran his fingers through his sleep tossed hair and added, "Geez it scared the crap out of me the way she bolted out of the room. I didn't know what was wrong at first."

"Glad I missed the show this time," Reed said. He grabbed another chair and moved it just far enough away from Nora that she wasn't on his lap.

"Scoot over," she said and shoved him playfully. "I want to breathe my own air!"

"Nope," he said in answer. Then he swung his arm over the back of her chair and inched it even closer to him, I'm sure, out of complete spite. Nora turned and frowned at him before pointedly looking away.

"So, what are the plans for the day?" Ash asked.

"I am going to get the garden up and running," I said. "Then I'm going to go see my wolves and talk to them."

Reed raised one eyebrow but didn't say a word. Ash, however, said, "Your wolves?"

"Yes," I said and tilted my head back to look him in the eye. "My wolves."

"Told you they'd be pets before the end of the week," Nora said to Reed.

"Don't think you will win any arguments over this one, dude," Reed said to Ash.

"Didn't plan on it," Ash said. "Just wanted clarification."

"I need to get some tech. Nora and I can go into town and pick up a few things. You can let me know if you need anything, and we can get it as well. I'm thinking we will need some type of secure internet connection along with a decent computer and set up."

"Works for me," Ash said. "I can help Eve. Not that she needs it, but if she does, I can help her get started. Is there anything you guys want me to do here while you are gone?"

"Nah," Reed said. "We can also pick up a pizza while we're in town. Nora needs to pick up her shirts and get her shift schedule."

"Cool. That good with you, Eve?" Ash asked.

"Yep. Just cheese for me please," I said.

"I'm going to get us some throw away phones too," Nora said. "Anything we had before is most likely compromised. I think a fresh start is the way to go."

I agreed with all of them, and what they were saying. I just had my mind already started on my garden. How to get it going and in the best order and form. I was also really hungry all of a sudden and was shuffling through my brain as to what all we'd bought from the grocery I could eat, fast.

I got up from Ash's lap and started nosing around in the cupboards. We'd gotten some chips. I knew we had. I opened one cabinet after another looking for them. They were fake processed cheese coated chips. They sounded good. Where were they?

"What are you looking for," Ash asked me.

I turned around and said, "The chips we got yesterday," only to find they were all staring at me. "What?" I asked.

"You good?" Nora asked.

"Yes, why?"

They all looked down at our feet.

I slowly looked down as well and found a coating of little delicate white and pink spring daisies carpeting the ground in a little path from the table to the cabinet. Not like a couple here and there either. Oh no. There was a literal covering of green leaves, stems, and little flowers in different stages of blooms.

I looked up at Ash who had the nerve to smile at me. I couldn't help myself. I started to laugh. Like fully belly, bend at the waist, laugh. Then Ash joined in, along with Reed and Nora.

"What are we going to do with all of them?" I asked after I had pulled myself together, but then I looked back down at my feet, with my toes curled in the greenery and I started laughing all over again.

Ash looked down at the floor, then got down on his knees to get a closer look. He grabbed a handful of the greenery and gave it a tug. It did pull out rather easily but there were still stems and roots in its place.

"Well, I think we can use a spade to scrape it off the floorboards, but I'm not sure what to do with the roots of them," Ash said.

I wondered if I could pull the energy away from them. Sort of a reverse of what I'd done to create them. "Let me try something."

"What are you thinking?" Nora asked.

"I'm going to try to remove the energy from them." I figured I'd given them life, maybe I could take it away too. I shivered, as a chill ran though my body at the thought of being a death bringer. Was that part of my gift, my powers? To take energy away and in effect kill? Was this how Reed felt?

Ash was suddenly at my side. Not hanging on me, just hovering. He'd obviously noticed I was upset. "I know you don't like the idea of killing your plants, but Eve, we can't keep them in the house like this. This isn't our house."

I shook my head and said, "It's not that. I understand we must get rid of them."

"Then what is it, honey," Nora asked coming up to stand with me as well.

"I was thinking about how to remove the daisies and then I thought, maybe as I'd used my spark of energy, granted without really knowing I was doing it, to create the flowers, maybe I could pull the energy away from them to make them die out."

"Okay, that's a great idea. What's the issue then," Reed asked in the very direct manner he had. It's a good thing I understood his mannerisms as it came across very rude.

"I always create life. I've never taken it away before. I've never been a bringer of death to things. I don't know how to deal with that," I said.

Nora rubbed my bare arm in a comforting way and said, "Have you ever tried to do that before? Take away energy?"

"No," I answered.

"So, that means you don't even know for certain if you can."

"Yeah," I said not understanding where she was going.

"How about before you decide to freak out about what you might be able to do, you see if you can. Then if you can, you can decide what to do about it." Nora had been spending a lot of time with Reed as her manner was a little more in your face than usual. She made perfect sense though. Even if there weren't any flowery words of comfort within her statement.

"Okay," I said with a nod of my head. I turned and looked at Ash and said, "Let's see what I can do then."

Ash didn't respond other than to give me a gentle squeeze in the form of a hug, for confidence.

I figured the simplest way was most likely the right way. So instead of pushing energy, I pulled it. I pulled it right back inside of myself. I don't really feel anything when I push energy out to use my gift. But, grabbing it back, was a whole other story. I could feel the energy as it gathered inside me. My body was vibrating with the excess load of it.

It was like my skin extended as I pulled the life back inside me. I watched as I am sure the others did as well, as the leaves and flowers bent, then curled, and finally browned and shriveled to ash and dust.

"Well, that ought to do it," Reed said.

"Just a sweep of the debris and it will be back to normal," Nora chimed in. "Nice job!"

I didn't have any words to respond with. I felt sad and at the same time energized with all the extra energy zipping around inside of me. My eyes were burning with unspent emotion, and I didn't want the others to see it. I quickly turned back to face the cupboard and said, "Now, where was I?"

In between chuckles, Ash said, "Future reference everyone, don't get in the way of Eve and her chips."

~ * ~

I stood outside in the heat of the day staring down at my lovely patch of earth that was ready for me to add some plants and life too. The sun was warm against my bare shoulders and legs. I took a short moment to tilt my head up, close my eyes, and just basked in the yellow brightness of the sun. Then, hands on hips I got to business.

We'd need easy plants like tomatoes, peppers, and lettuce. But we could also use different types of potatoes and melon. Not the fancy ones, just standard watermelon and maybe cantaloupe. Then we'd need the squash. The usual cucumbers and zucchini, but also a few fun ones like acorn, butternut, and spaghetti.

I stopped there for a moment to decide if I wanted the peas and beans too and decided…why not. I'd need a few trellis items for them to climb, but they would add to what we could sell and what we could eat. Who doesn't like a good green bean or garden pea?

With my items determined, I pulled out the seeds I had gotten the day before and got down to business.

"Hey! Don't start without me," Ash yelled from the house.

"Then hurry up!" I shouted back and then didn't wait at all and just began the fun and relaxing task of bringing life to the earth in the form of veggies and fruits.

This was the best part of my gift. Watching the ground go from empty to full of life and growth and color. Green and yellows, reds, and oranges. I put a seed in a small hole I'd poked in the ground, and then covered it with dirt. Then I covered that spot with my hands and pushed. Not physically push down, but mentally push out life energy from within me. I focused on the seed I couldn't see but knew was there, and after a moment, I could feel a little sprout tickling my palm as it tried to make its way up. I moved my palm out from in its way, and then pushed a bit more until a nice plant was in the works.

I sat back on my heels and inspected my little pepper plant. It stood about a foot tall, had wide deep green leaves, and a handful of little closed up flowers waiting to open. I gave a nod of approval and stood up. One plant down. How many more to go? It didn't matter how many more as I loved every moment of it.

Ash did help out by building me some climbing trellis out of a few poles and some string he'd found in the storage shed. They would be perfect and not something I could just create with my energy. It was good to work beside him.

We didn't have to talk or really engage at all as we knew each other well enough to work and work together without words. I sat down right on the ground where I'd been working on building up a hill of potatoes. I swiped a bead of sweat off my forehead and turned to watch Ash.

He was also feeling the heat as he'd taken off his shirt and was working in nothing but his shorts. The muscles on his arms flexed with the work while the sweat added a sheen thanks to the sun. I moved on to watch his chest as it contracted under the force of his task.

He must have felt my gaze as he stopped and gave me a hard look. "You good? You ready for a break?"

I don't know what possessed me other than the sight of him working next to me in the hot light of day, and knowing we had the house to ourselves for a while, but I tossed him what I thought of as a sultry smile and slowly, slowly stood up to face him.

His eyebrows lifted and a matching smile hit his face. The shovel he'd been using hit the ground as he swooped me up and tossed me over his shoulder. He then turned and headed toward the house and to the confines of our room where he slowly but completely, and with my full cooperation, took advantage of the quiet moment of aloneness.

Just before I fell to sleep, and while our bodies were still damp, he said, "You have no idea how much I love you."

But I did. I was certain it was on the same level of how much I loved, adored, and craved him. We were the perfect match.

Neither of us looked outside or had any notion that during our little afternoon interlude, my freshly planted garden, was now in full and colorful bloom. No, there were not any fruits or veggies yet, but the plants had grown without any intentional effort by me.

After our nap as Ash and I were out marveling at my garden, Reed and Nora returned. "Wow, nice work Eve! That looks awesome." Nora said.

She was carrying a few green shirts, which I assumed was her pizza place outfit. Reed, however, was bogged down with a ton of bags and boxes. "Dude, a little help?"

Ash went over and took some of the bags from Reed and together they went into the house. "Don't expect to see either of them for a while," Nora said. She'd come to where I was in the garden and plopped down on the ground in the cool shade of the tree.

"Why?" I asked her, as I watched their trek from the car to the house.

"Reed spent a fortune on computer crap. I am not a techie, but I am not tech stupid either and I have no idea what half that stuff is he bought."

"I admit to not being techie. I'm more…organic," I said and meant it. Aside from a cell phone and maybe an email here and there, I had no real interest in it. Don't get me wrong, I know how useful and necessary it could be, especially, for us as we hunted for answers, but I preferred what I could sink my hands into instead of my brain.

"Honestly, me too. Aside from old cars though. I do like playing with them," she said smiling more to herself and what she was seeing in her own mind, than at me.

"You mean stealing them," I said and laughed.

She didn't get upset, in fact she simply shrugged and said, "There is that. Stealing is definitely, fun."

"You good out here?" she asked.

"Yeah. I'm going to go check on my wolves," I said as I got up and brushed off the back of my shorts.

"Where are they?"

I nodded to the fields behind the shed. "Just over there a bit."

"They're really close," she said a little cautiously.

I shrugged. "Maybe a bit, but they seem to feel better when they can stay closer to the house, and I guess me."

"You need me to stay? Come with you?"

"Nah. I'm good," I said and headed in the direction I'd indicated.

"Call out if you need us," she said.

I tossed a wave at her and moved on. My wolves were just where I said they'd be. Not all of them. Only about seven of the pack. I moved in toward them. I sent out little energy feelers, and they all seemed okay with my being there.

The big male stood up from where he laid in a patch of sun within the group, as I drew closer. He met me a few feet from where the others still rested. He bumped his head on my leg in a sort of greeting. It also felt like he was telling the others I was not a threat. They must have trusted him as they didn't get up or move at all really.

I dropped a light hand on his head and then reminded myself he was not a pet and was in fact wild. He likely didn't need or want me caressing him. His fur under my hand though was warm from the sun and crisp in texture.

I left my hand on his head, and as gently as I could pushed into his mind. He flinched away from me for a second, but then settled back down. I had wanted to see if they could help find out if there were graves around the old compound we'd burnt down. I could tell the big wolf didn't like the idea of death. Natural part of life or not he had an aversion to it. I felt and tried to understand what he was conveying, and I realized he and the others knew what death smelled like and where some animals may crave the smell, the death I was looking for, did not come with a smell they liked. It was not normal. It smelled bad.

I pressed into him that we needed to know where the death that smelled off was located. Could they find it and show us?

He stepped away from me and looked into my eyes with his deep brown ones. I was trying to grow a bond with the wolves, but it felt like maybe I was rushing it a bit. I'd have to try again another time. He was starting to give me his trust and I didn't want to ruin that. I sent back to him I was trusting him too.

I wanted their help to find the graves because I wanted to try to find out who or what was in them. What SaneCorp was doing. After Ash had found the dismembered girl that had signs of being one of us, I couldn't let the thought of it go. It worried me. What was SaneCorp making? What would we be facing in the future if they succeeded.

Although I could feel the big wolf's desire to help, he and the pack were not ready. We would just have to wait and see what the pack would do.

The male left my side, settled back into his sunspot, closed his eyes, and relaxed into a summer doze. I sent out a goodbye to them all and went back home to tell the others how it went.

Chapter Six

The days and weeks passed. Nora got started at her job at the pizza place. She probably wouldn't admit it, but I think she enjoyed it. She had a lot of regulars come in specifically when she was working. She made good tips, which I know made her feel like she was contributing. She was good at it, and it showed. Plus, we got a lot of free food. That was a huge perk we had not anticipated. Subs, pizza, garlic bread, and salad. The free food was a definite bonus.

Reed went to work at a small computer shop in town. He also enjoyed it, but it was not because of the people. He just liked doing that type of work. Thinking about how to fix the tech and get it running better, faster, and cheaper. According to Reed, the people didn't really like him.

I think they were scared of him. He was no longer sporting the shaved head, but even with the dark hair covering his head, which did give him a softer appearance, he could be scary when he stared you down with his intense steely eyes. However, even if the customers were not all that comfortable around him, he was a standard request for service tech on most, if not all, computer type issues. Scary or not, he did a good job, and everyone knew it.

Ash found a job at a motorcycle place. It was right in town, only about a block away from where the farmer's market was held. Funny how that worked out. He was loving it. He got to ride a lot of bikes. According to him it was just for test driving purposes, but he loved it. That kick of adrenaline he got when he could set those wheels racing down a back road, yeah, he loved it. The people liked him well enough too and asked for him especially. He was a techie like Reed and could have worked with him at the computer store, but there really is only so much work in a small town. Plus, they saw one another enough every day. I'm sure some time away was good for us all.

Me? I did what I always do. I set up in town at the local farmer's market. Everyone would come and help get me set up each day before they went off on their own. I mingled and formed relationships with all the other vendors. I learned the people in town. I got to know faces and had my own regulars who asked for certain things. My produce sold like crazy. I'm not surprised, as it was grown to be big and tasty. Plus, as I didn't have to put as much time, energy, or money into growing mine, I made a hefty profit every day.

The baby was growing. I tried to keep any touch of energy very light when I did reach out. I always just touched to make sure all was well, then I moved away. I wasn't showing much yet either. Maybe a little tummy but it didn't look like a baby was in there. I looked like I'd eaten a big meal. I wanted a baby belly, a big one to show off and be proud of. I also knew the longer it took to show, the better off we'd all be.

"Hey you!" Connie Price said, walking over from her stall that contained mountains of bread. She was my favorite stall. I have a thing for bread. I just do.

"Hey! How's business?" I asked her back.

"Good. Not as good as yours. I thought while there was a lull, I better come say hello and buy my own produce before it was all gone! You sure do have a green thumb."

I smiled a real smile at her. I loved her stall because of the bread, but I really enjoyed her too as she seemed like good people. "What do you need? We can trade. I have a hankering for your cheddar jalapeño bread."

"One loaf of bread won't be a fair trade for what I want from your stand," she said with a chuckle.

"Well, tell me what you want, and we can figure out how to make it even." Having a chance to get more bread than just the cheddar bread, oh I was down for that! I always loved bread, but lately, it seemed more like a need. I smiled thinking about the little life inside me, demanding warm yeasty and a bit spicy, cheese bread.

"So, can I ask you something?" she asked.

I was immediately on edge, but I put a warm smile on my face and said, "Sure."

"I know we aren't supposed to ask this question anymore as its considered rude, but it's kinda my thing. So, you can't get offended."

"Okay," I said. A wiggly feeling began in the pit of my stomach, as I worried what was on her mind.

"Well, are you expecting?"

I huffed out a surprised laugh that was part relief and still part fear. "How can you tell? I didn't think I was showing or anything." Cause if I was showing, I needed to take more precautions. SaneCorp and all its minions had been awful quiet lately, but quiet didn't mean they were gone.

"Oh, no. You aren't showing or anything like that. I meant what I said. It's sorta my thing. I just, know when a woman is expecting. It's my one psychic ability," she said with an embarrassed smile and laugh. Probably expecting me to laugh at her and not with her.

"Well, that is quite the gift," I said and meant it. "How could you tell though?"

She pursed her lips and then said, "My daughter says its gross."

Now I really needed to know. I laughed and said, "What?"

"Okay," she said and lowered her voice a bit. "It's two things. The first is that women who are carrying, put off a bit of glow. It's like a warmth that comes off them."

"Okay, but that's not gross."

"No, but it's weird. I know not everyone can see it. I thought it was a usual thing for women to be able to see it, but apparently, it's not. I'm broken."

I was already shaking my head at her before she finished speaking. "You are not broken, that is awesome."

"The weird and gross part is, that pregnant women also put off a scent. A sickly-sweet smell I pick up on. It's not a bad or a yuck thing. It is just like a sugary thing. That smell, coupled with the little glow, and I know when someone is pregnant."

"I would never think to tell anyone they are weird. Of all people, I'm a little weird on my own, so I like the un-normal people. I think it makes them amazing. So, if you have this talent, then I am going to cheer you on for it from the sidelines." I meant it too. It's hard being thought of as a freak.

I had been a freak my whole life. My parents, well, at first, they liked my abnormal. Praised it and thanked their god for it. Then not so much.

They began to fear it and fear me. I was not ever going to do that to someone who had a natural special talent. Ever.

Connie seemed a little uncomfortable with my words, so I changed the subject. "I didn't know you had a daughter. I know you have your son, Scotty, but not a daughter."

Her face fell.

"Oh, I'm sorry. Did I say something wrong?" I asked, placing my hand on her arm. I didn't mean to, and I wasn't trying to intrude but I got a huge kick in the chest of sad energy that just pushed off her and into me. I kept my face the same and tried not to show the effect her little burst of emotion had on me.

The effect was harsh too. Heavy and so sad and broken. I wanted to cry for it, for her. She had been so happy and carefree but a moment before and now, just heartbroken.

"No, no. It's nothing you said. My daughter and I had a fight about a year and half ago. She packed up a bag and said she was leaving and going to New York. She did, and I haven't heard from her since."

"That's awful. Have you tried to get ahold of her?" I asked.

"That's the funny thing. The fight wasn't a relationship ending kind of thing. We were just arguing over her future and what plans she had. I thought going off to New York with little to no money was a dumb idea. She said her future lay in the night lights and she was going. I figured she'd get there and stumble a bit, but she's at least call me, and I could, I don't know, send her money. Talk her through whatever was going on. But I've not heard a peep from her."

"Is that like her?" I asked, getting my own bad feelings over her story.

She shook her head and said, "No. It's not. She and I are close. We have never gone a week without talking before this and now…it's been what seems like forever."

I didn't know what to say so I just left my hand on her arm, giving her what little comfort I could.

We stayed like that for a moment, then she sorta shook it off and said, "That's okay. I like to picture her in my head living the high life in New York. Making a name for herself. She'll call me just as soon as she can prove me wrong." She smiled a sort of sad smile, but one I was sure she used as a way to convince others she was fine.

Something about her story hit me wrong though. Did she run away? It was possible, but it was even more likely she was taken. I had an awful idea of who she was taken by too. There was an easy way to find out. "What was her name?"

"Cheryl Ann," she said. "She hated it, and went by Ann instead, but that was her given name. Cheryl Ann Price."

"Well, I will think of her in New York too. Her hair lit by the city lights at night. Her days spent in luxury." I chuckled at the idea of a young and fresh-faced girl making it in the big city.

I was not a big fan of New York City. It was so loud and crowded. Now that I understood better some of my gifts, I realized part of my dislike of the place was the negative energy that seemed to abound there. At least in the parts of the city I could afford to be in, back then when I was young and broke, as they were not the great parts. Maybe the places with the big bright lights were better.

"Ope, I have a customer. I better get back to it. I'll come by in a bit and get my order in before it's all gone!" She sent a wave over her shoulder as she headed back to her stall. "I'll put aside a cheddar loaf for you!"

Even though I sent her a wave and a smile, my brain was already racing with thoughts on what I could even do if I found Ann's name on the list. Would her mom want to know? Plus depending on what list, she was on…would depend on if she was missing, unknown, or dead. I didn't know if it was better to believe your child was just living a grand life in the city or if it was better to know she was dead and not coming back. Ever.

At five, I began to pack up what little I had left for the day. Ash and Nora arrived together a few minutes later. "How was work?" I asked them both.

Nora lifted her shoulders and let them drop in an exaggerated fashion, and said, "Living the dream." Then she gave me a huge smile and said, "Actually, it kinda is right? We get to get up and live our days exactly as we please. I have a family now who takes me as I am and isn't afraid of me. We have money and freedom, and even though we know the lull in the storm won't last forever, it is a wonderful lull."

"Dude, where did that come from?" Ash asked with a confused look on his face. "You get a rainbow shoved up you somewhere today?"

A burst of laugher escaped in shock and surprise at Ash's question. "Ash! Oh my gosh!"

Nora just laughed right in his face and said, "Yeah. I did. I had a great day. Made good tips. Talked to my regulars. It was a perfect day for me."

She was a little on the chipper side. That was a bit strange for her as she tended to be more reserved and sarcastic. Loved her for it, but this happy person was not the normal Nora we all knew. So, even I had to ask, "You good?"

Connie ran up just then with her arms loaded down with different types of bread, including my coveted cheddar jalapeño loaf. "I didn't forget you!" She handed her load off to Ash and then did a double take at Nora. "Uh…" she stuttered then looked at me with a bit of a strange look.

I took control of the moment completely unsure what was going on in the undercurrents other than Nora was genuinely feeling happy which was strange, and Connie had this feeling of surprise and uncertainty around her. "I have your box here too. I put some extras in, as they will go to waste if someone doesn't take them. I won't be back until Friday, and they won't be fresh by then. If you can't use them, maybe pass them on to someone that can."

Connie took her box full of produce and said, "Okay. Thanks!" Then, "Have you been to the OB yet?"

I hadn't as I wasn't sure if I was going to be like the normal pregnant ladies. I was afraid she would question me about things I couldn't share. Plus, was my blood even normal? Were my other stats? I'd never been to a regular doctor before. Ever. "Not yet. We haven't been in town long enough for me to see who is good."

"Well, you have to go see Ellen." She turned and looked at Nora again and smiled when she said, "She's the best you will find. She could give you a checkup too in case you needed it." The last part she directed at Nora.

I focused on Nora then. Hard. "Oh my God!" I hadn't meant to say anything. It just sorta slipped out. I felt it. I knew. Nora had a little spark of life inside her. Small. Barely there at all, but Connie saw it for what it was.

Ash turned and took hold of my arm. "What? Are you okay?"

I turned away from Nora and Connie and worked to get my face into a semblance of normal as I was sure I presented as utter shocked and surprised. "Yes. Just had a moment there. I'm good."

"Are you sure?" Ash was concerned. Since I was tapping into everyone's energy better, I could get more emotional information from anyone I centered on.

Knowing he was upset and worried, I smiled and gave him a quick kiss at the corner of his mouth and said, "I'm sure. I'm great. I promise."

I was too. Nora was barely there, but she had a life growing in her. My little one would not be alone in this world as the only altered human or maybe we should be meta humans, whatever you called us, the babies would not be alone in the world. Was it selfish to want that? Maybe. But that was how I felt all the same.

I was not going to share my insight with Nora either. She would have to figure it out herself and then tell us when she was ready. I was not going to ruin that moment for her or Reed for that matter. Oh, it was going to be wonderful! I wanted to do a little dance right there, but I was certain the others would not know what to do with me.

After we said our goodbyes to Connie and the rest of the usual market people, we hauled our stuff back to the car.

"I see we had another good day," Ash said.

"Made a nice chunk of change too, to go with it," I added in. "I know you guys have quite the stash of funds put aside, but it makes me feel better to have money coming in."

"Me too," Nora said.

Once we were settled in our car and headed back home, I told them about the conversation I'd had with Connie about her daughter Cheryl Ann. "I want us to go through our lists and see if she's on them."

"Then what?" Nora asked.

I shrugged and turned to face her where she sat in the back seat. "I don't know. I can't decide if it is kinder to let it be and not tell her anything or if it would be better for her know so she can stop wondering and worrying."

"We can decide together once we know if she's on the lists or not," Ash said.

"Plus, we can determine if the company really was using town people for their experiments. I feel like we've put it off long enough. It's time to get into the reason we decided to stay here. One to determine if all the missing people in town were due to SaneCorp. Two, to determine the ones that are not towns people and determine where they originate from. Three, to determine if the people found in any mass graves are on any of the lists. Fourth and final, to determine what they were doing with them and their experiments."

Nora pulled a face and said, "I can't tell you how long it took after seeing that body buried in the shed to get rid of the nightmares. The fact it was in pieces and parts and not all of her pieces and parts were in there. I mean, where was the rest of her?" She gave a quick shiver almost as if to punctuate her words.

"Thanks for the reminder of that visual!" I said and gave a small shiver of my own.

"How do you think I feel?" Ash asked. "She was like me with the little starter areas on her hand and who really knows where else. Plus, the idea she had been mutated not as an egg, but as a fully formed human. That's scary as hell!"

Actually, what I thought was really scary was whether or not their experiment worked, but if it did why tear her apart like they had and why had they kept the pieces they did? The ones we'd found in the shed. What was so important about those parts that they didn't get rid of them?

Finally, home, Nora went directly inside. I assume to find Reed. Ash and I unloaded what little was left from the days sales. Then we went inside with my bread haul to find the others and touch base on our day.

After we'd all caught up on the minutia, Ash asked Reed how the computer center we'd been creating in the house was coming along. The guys had gone out several times to get different things. Cords or drives or monitors. You name it we probably now had it in our shared living space.

"Actually, I spent a lot of time inputting the data from all those different lists we've found and cross referenced them with different aspects. I think we have a good idea of who, what, when, and where now."

"Ooo then can you do a search on a name?" I asked. Maybe this could be the start of figuring out the rest of our lives. I know. I know. One name won't be the thing that sets us free forever, but it could be the one thing that starts the avalanche toward that freedom.

"Yep, I'm ready," Reed said from where he sat at what was once a giant dining room table now turned into a computer table. There were three monitors set up in a curved viewing pattern along with a laptop and what I know as a desktop computer system. There were also stand-alone drives and a bowl full of jump drives each named with a number.

I had no idea what the numbering system indicated but Reed and Ash obviously did. Finally, there was a lot of all this different but necessary junk, as I called it. A big mat that was like three feet wide and long was used for the mouse. There were spiral notebooks and a cup of pens, pencils, highlighters, binder clips, folders, paper clips. You name it, they probably bought it. It was a lot of stuff. There was even a printer sitting on the floor under the table.

I was told it was a laser jet color and was one of the best. My thoughts were…ok. Great.

I gave him Cheryl Ann's full name and he put it into a search. There was a status bar slowly progressing and then, her name came up in a listing Reed had created from all the lists we had gathered.

Next to her name it had the letters D U I. I pointed at them and asked, "What do the letters mean?"

Reed spun around to face us and explained, "There were several references on the lists we obtained."

"Stole," Ash said with a grin.

I turned to frown at him. I liked the word obtained better and he knew it.

Reed ignored Ash completed and continued on with his explanation, "The D U I stand for dead upon injection. So, I assume they died right as they were given whatever they were being injected with. Then there was D A I which is dead after injections, so those ones must have been ones that survived the initial jab but died soon thereafter. The last set, is just terminated."

"Terminated? Liked killed?" Nora asked. It was a question, but it was also a statement. Putting it out there in a way to express that we all knew that killed is exactly what it meant.

"Yeah, but I don't know the why or the when. They survived the injection and then what? They didn't live up to expectations, so they were destroyed. Or they did and they wanted to study them from the inside to see how it worked so they were terminated to be autopsied? These are questions I don't have the answers too."

"That's a bit disappointing," Nora said.

I agreed. What did we actually know? "So, there are no known successes?"

"Not that I see from the data we have."

"Is that good or bad do you think?" Ash asked.

Reed shrugged and I had to agree with that too. Did we want any successes out there in the world like we were? No. Did we want any successes to be killed just for the studying of them? Again, no. A shrug was the perfect answer to the question.

"So, we know Cheryl Ann died from the injection," I stated.

"Yep, of a serum called Serum 19," Reed said.

"I wonder what number they're on now," Ash said.

"I guess we can assume the girl in the shed was a failure in some fashion and was likely terminated for scientific study. She had clear signs of mutation, but we don't know if it was the right mutation or the wrong one, only that they chopped her up to study her more," Reed added.

The idea of that girl being cut up and thrown away turned my stomach. I must have made a face as Ash said, "Sorry, babe. Moving on."

"What should we do next?" I asked.

"What do you mean?" Reed asked.

"I mean now what? Can you tell which ones on the list are from town and the missing? Who is everyone? Is that one reporter, you remember her, Heather something? Is she on the list? I mean now what?"

"I think our next step is to make sure there aren't any people on the lists that are not on the terminated or dead list. Then we will know if there are leftovers that could be, like us."

"Then what?" I asked again.

"Eve, what are you wanting to be next?" Ash asked. He came over to me, took my hand in his warm one, and gave me his undivided attention.

"I want it to end," I said and then promptly burst into tears. Unexpected and although not especially out of the ordinary, this was not one of the times I would generally have been in tears.

Ash's eyes went wide. Nora and Reed looked as confused as I felt. "I'm sorry. I don't know why I'm so upset. I do want all this," I said not even sure what all this was, "to end. I'm tired. I am afraid for our children. I'm afraid for the possible new mutants out there."

Thankfully, my tears ended as quickly as they started. Now I was moving away from sad to just angry. I really was tired of it all. I wanted a normal and simple life. My plants and animals. My children. No more running.

"Wait…children?" Ash said. "What does that mean?"

I back peddled a little bit, but my answer was the truth. "I plan on having more than one child. I plan on having at least a handful of them. So yeah, children. Maybe not today but more than one. Besides, Nora and Reed might have kids one day too."

"Not hardly!" Nora almost shouted. "I can barely take care of myself. How am I supposed to take care of a baby?"

Reed took that idea much better than Nora. "Eh, I wouldn't mind a little wind maker."

I pointed at Reed and said, "Exactly! Children."

"Good luck with that, buddy!" Nora said.

It took everything in me not to laugh. Nora was in for a shocker then. From tears, to anger, to laughter in the end. I must be tired in more ways than one.

Ash took the reins of the conversation and moved away from children. "Okay, we are all feeling that way but what do you want to do about it?"

"I think, we should stop trying to do away with these little off branches of SaneCorp. I think we should take the company on as whole. Get them shut down and the powers at the top…no longer in power of any kind."

"Destroy them from top to bottom," Nora said. "Yeah, I like that." A gleeful smile bloomed across her face. It was a little disconcerting, but then again, that was Nora.

"Take the fight to them," Reed added and nodded his head. Reed wasn't the big toothy smile type, but he did give a grin. His smile was more than disconcerting, it was dark and scary, but hey, you get what you get.

"Which brings us to the question of how we do that?" Ash asked.

Reed answer. "I've been giving this some thought too. I think we get as much information as we can on all these test subjects. Find out who they are and where they are from. Then we can leak what we know to the news. Not just locally either. Nationwide. Any place a group of people are from, we can send out a sort of media packet."

"They can just squash the story. They are big enough," Nora said.

Nora tended to always bring negative energy…I tried not to sigh. I tried not to get annoyed. "Not if we send it everywhere. There will be some of the media companies that get the story out fast and others will be forced to pick it up, pay out, or not."

"They will come for us. They will come for you and the baby," Nora replied.

"They are always going to be in the background of our lives unless we do something about it. This is something. Why are you so against it?"

"Because!" she all but shouted. "We are doing well here. We have lives. We have each other. I don't want to mess it up and have them coming for us again."

I stepped over to her and took her hands in mine, then said, "Nora, we all have something to lose if we go after them. But you also know we will never be free, never be able to put aside that feeling in the back of our minds and in our hearts that we are not safe. We won't ever be safe and free until they are gone. I know we have set up a nice life today. But, what about tomorrow. What about those future children? Will they thank us for their lives if they are living the same ones we are living today? Scared? Running?"

"You girls need to get control of your powers. Just saying," Reed said.

Nora and I both let go of each other and looked around us. It was snowing. Not hard, just fat little flakes drifting down around us to land…on a carpet of spring daisies under our feet that had not been there a moment before.

Now I did sigh, big and out loud. There was another mess I was going to have to clean up.

Nora and I both seemed to take a breath and let out our fear. Then we laughed at the consequences of our emotions. "Why does that keep happening?" I said in between laughter.

Ash decided to laugh along with us. "I get why you are having a little trouble regulating but not Nora. Dude, what's with your girl?"

Reed was nice and flipped Ash off in response.

"Excuse the hell out of me for being emotional about my life. I forgot, you boys aren't supposed to have any feeling or emotions. My bad," Nora snarked.

I wrapped my arm around Nora's and together we headed out of the computer room dining room area and went into the kitchen. "I'm hungry. Let's get something to eat," I said.

That night after dinner, the four of us sat at the kitchen table to discuss our plan of action. Everyone had come around to my way of thinking. It was nothing I did to them. I think everyone just realized I was right. We would never be completely free until SaneCorp was gone. Gone for good.

"We got more data than just the people list, right?" Nora asked.

"Yeah, we did. I just wasn't focused on it until now. I had been trying to work through all the different spreadsheets and lists we had gotten and put them in some semblance of order we could filter through. Now that that issue is done, Ash and I can start digging into the other data we have. See what it actually gives us."

"Okay," I said.

"We can also make sure the media data we have is sent out on the SaneCorp letterhead so when we send them out into the world, they are taken more seriously, than just chucks of data might be," Reed said.

"Okay, what can we do to help?" I asked.

"Since we want to work on the other data, you and Nora can start going through the people data and determining who is local and who is not. Who they are. Like do they still have family here? What is their story? Then the others that are not local you can do the same," Ash said.

"What will that accomplish?" I asked.

"With that information, we can make sure to focus our media blitz on the companies that have high levels of local people. For instance, we go to the town newspapers and local television stations with all the information on the people from that area. That will hit home more than someone they don't know who is from across the country."

That was a great idea. "Okay," I said and looked at Nora for confirmation. "We can do that!"

"Yeah, I'm in," Nora said. "Taking it to the personal level is a great idea. It might get our story more traction if it hits home."

"Can we set our media package up in a way no one will know they come from us? The leak is anonymous?" I asked. I was all for going after them, but I didn't want a giant bullseye on us either.

"You doubt our skills?" Ash said with mock indignation. His eyes were wide, his hand was over his heart. "How could you!"

I rolled my eyes so far back, I'm certain I almost saw my own brain. Nora must have felt the same as she said, "Whatever."

Chapter Seven

I stood at my stall at the farmer's market, feeling a bit sorry for myself. I sighed as I was alone, once again. I know each of us had our own things to do and places to work, I did. I just thought they would come and share the time with me a little. Instead, they always had their own places to go and stuff they wanted or needed to get to.

They did help me set up each day. They seemed to be taking turns. I was getting to the point where I didn't even need that. Okay I needed it as I didn't want to be lifting supper heavy bins, but it felt like such a trial some days as they would pretty much just dump the bins at my spot, make sure I had my canopy up and set, and then they would be like, "see you later." They would head out fast, leaving me to fend for myself. I sighed again.

I was fine on my own. I mean, it wasn't like I didn't have people I could talk to. Connie was across from me, one, two, three stands down. We could wave to each other but couldn't really talk unless one of us left our stand. When it was busy, we couldn't do that.

Directly across from me was the salsa guy. I think his name was Tim. He was friendly enough but also a bit territorial, so I didn't talk to him much other than the daily good morning, or how's it going?

Next to him was the dog treat lady. She was nice. Her name was Crystal. She didn't have any children but had a ton of dogs. Hence her desire to make dog centered food and treats.

Down the way was a little old man named, Ken. He sold eggs. I didn't have the heart to tell him I thought his chickens were sick. The eggs gave me a weird feeling. I knew they were okay, but not really up to par. I stayed away from the eggs and Ken, so I didn't have to worry about it.

As I surveyed the market that day, I realized I was getting a weird feeling. A watched feeling by someone angry or unhappy. Dangerous maybe? I did a little check in with each of the stalls around me and it was not the venders.

From there I started gently touching each shopper with my energy. It is amazing what you can find out about someone if you can see inside them. One lady was sad, broken. But her outward appearance was happy and content. She put on a great emotional mask. There was a little boy bouncing around at the side of an older lady. Grandma maybe? He was excited and giddy. Maybe because he knew grandma would buy him something. Each person I could pick out little things about them. However, none of them felt dangerous.

Then I landed on a man. Tall. Beefy arms and legs but slim everywhere else. He fit in nicely with everyone in a pair of old jeans and a well-worn and likely loved t-shirt. His brown hair was short but not military short. His eyes I couldn't see yet, but they were hard and focused on me. He was surveying me as I was him.

I was immediately concerned. Not scared, but definitely not happy. He was heading on a direct course to my table. I looked over at Connie, thinking maybe I could just bounce over to her table for a moment, but she was busy with customers.

The man arrived at my stall. He stood across the table from me. Close enough I could see his eyes were bright light blue. Icy and cold. I held back a shiver, even though it was quite warm outside. This man was one to be aware of and I was nervous around him but not exactly scared. I tried to feel him out, but all I got was unhappy. No. Not unhappy. Not exactly. Scared and maybe anxious.

We stared at one another for a long minute. Neither of us saying anything, until he finally said, "You have a nice stand here. Lots of produce that looks to be at peak ripeness. In fact, I don't see one bad piece of anything."

I shrugged at him and said, "I leave those ones at home. I only bring the best to the market."

He then stuck out his hand and said, "My name's Tom."

I did not want to touch this man. The emotional feel of him from a distance was hard enough, but it would be ten times worse if I actually touched him. I hesitated and tried to find a way out of it, without seeming to.

Then the issue was solved for me as an arm reached around me and took hold of Tom's outstretched hand and said, "I'm Connie. It's nice to meet you. Are you new to town or just passing through?"

The complete and utter annoyance that passed over his features before he was able to wipe them away and produce a smile I could see right through, was almost comical. "Not passing through but not really staying either. I'm here for a few weeks maybe. It depends on how long it takes," he said and turned to face me to finished, "for me to complete the job I'm here for."

"What job is that?" Connie asked.

"Research and acquisition," he said dryly.

I bet I knew exactly what he was trying to acquire. This was not good. I tried to gently reach out to gauge him with my energy, but all I got was emotions. Nothing concrete on what he wanted or who he was. My gifts were awesome most of the time. In this, they were a little limited.

"Well, nice to meet you. I need to get back over to my table. Come say hello and get some bread before you head out." She left with a wave over her shoulder at us both, but I still felt her absence as she left me alone with Tom.

He put his hand back out again and said, "Sorry, I didn't catch your name."

I stared at his hand again. There had to be a reason he was so insistent on touching me. Shaking my hand. I thought he was possibly a SaneCorp goon which made me wonder if he was mutated or not. I sure as heck was not laying one single finger on him. I picked up a handful of big zucchinis, lifted them toward him, and said with a huge friendly smile, "How rude of me. Can I offer something? These are as fresh as they come."

He slowly lowered his hand, and giving me a hard look, said, "No. Not Today."

"Well, as you said, I have the freshest produce in town. You make sure to come back and see me if you want anything veggie wise," I added still with the smile plastered on my face.

He opened his mouth as if to say something else, but thankfully and with perfect timing Jim, a regular customer dropped over and said, "Hey, missy! You have any of those giant tomatoes you had last week? Martha wants at least three if you do."

I turned fully toward Jim and said, "Of course I do!" I set down the squash, pulled out a little paper sack and began filling it with the requested tomatoes. I kept up a constant conversation with Jim, paying no obvious attention to Tom. Oh, I was very aware of every breath he took, but I didn't show it. "How are the kids? Is Emmy getting better at first base?"

"She got moved to short stop. She likes that spot better, so it's all good. I didn't know girls softball was so competitive for eight-year-olds."

I laughed and was about to respond when Tom cut in and said, "I'll be back later." It was normal easy words, but the weight behind them was not. It was a real threat and one I was well aware of. I just smiled his way and gave a small wave. I watched him from the corner of my eye as he made his way out of the market area. Only then did I take a deep breath and calm down. "I'm glad to hear it. Here you go," I said and handed him his bag. "Do you need anything else?"

"Not today. How much?" he asked as he dug out his wallet.

"Six please," I said.

He handed over his money, and with a wave of his own said, "See you Saturday!"

Saturday being the next market day. It was the day the entire family tended to come and do their shopping though. Most families came in groups on Saturdays. It was a big sale day for all of us. "I'll watch for you."

As Jim walked away, I picked back up the zucchinis I'd pulled out and turned to put them back only to find, my feet buried in…spring daisies. I sighed. What was up with that? Seriously.

When I saw Ash later that day, he asked his usual, "How was the day?"

I don't know why I didn't mention Tom, but I simply said as usual too, "It was fine."

As most of the produce was gone, he could see it was a good sales day. We both knew that was not what he was asking, but for once I kept a secret from him. Maybe it was because I was pretending to myself, we were still safe, and we were still okay here in this little town. I knew we had plans to take on SaneCorp, but we hadn't done anything to them yet. So, we should be okay, right? I pretended to myself that was true.

The next day was one of the days there was no market. Fridays were great days for me as I got to play out in the dirt with my plants and soak up the sun. My hands were deep in the dirt, my feet were bare and just as deep in the earth as my hands were. My bare knees were coated in it too. If I had to guess, I'd bet there was even some on my face.

It was a great morning. Yes, I'd still been sick first thing. Yes, I had to go have a nap afterward. After that though, I had a big breakfast, and here I was outside in jean shorts, a red tank top, with my hair piled up in a giant messy bun, basking in the vitamin D rich sunshine. I took a deep breath to just immerse myself in it.

I sensed my little wolf pack over in the forest again to the north. They were also enjoying the gorgeous day. If I could control the weather, it'd be hard to not give myself days like that all the time. I guess that is a good reason for me to not be able to control it.

"We meet again," a dark voice said from not but a few feet away from me. I knew that voice. How had I not sensed him before he got that close to me? That was a very real worry. I should have felt him long before he got to our place, let alone behind me. I slowly, and with extreme calm, got to my feet and turned to face Tom.

He was standing in a pair of dark jeans, and an old band T-shirt. The shirt was stretched tight over his chest. I'd say it was on purpose to show off his pecks and heavy muscles. It wasn't attractive to me. I'm sure it was to others, but I didn't get that from him. This man was big and felt dangerous to me. That was likely due to the very real fact that Ash, Reed, and Nora were all in town at their own jobs. I was alone.

I don't know what it was about him that sent my heart pounding as he didn't make a move toward me. He wasn't aggressive in any way. Why was I so unsettled?

"I want to talk to you. That's all I want," he said, but he again held out his hand to me. "Come on, Evie."

I heard what he said. Come on, Evie. It echoed in my head.

Come on, Evie. There was something I should have known. I could feel a nagging in my brain, that I should, and it was important, but I didn't. I just couldn't reach what I needed to know.

Come on, Evie… I closed my eyes and put a hand to my forehead. The nagging something was pounding. No, the pounding in my head was fear and it was real.

Come on, Evie…

I didn't sense him coming over to me. However, when he gently took my hand into his, I was very aware of him. Especially, as the moment we touched, a burst of energy exploded out from us in all directions. It was a pulse of heavy hard energy that shot out away from me in an invisible wave.

"Evie?" Tom said, and there was emotion behind it. Concern? Fear? Why?

I also knew the name Tom as not real. He was not a Tom. His name was… "Lark?"

The moment I said the name out loud he smiled. A real smile. I only had a second to notice it as my brain crashed down on me with pain. It was as if something was trying to break through, but it couldn't. There was a gate there holding everything back. The pressure behind the gate grew and grew and it was overwhelming.

I pulled my hand away from Lark, and grabbed my head, my hair crunched up in my fists at the same time. I dropped to my knees and tried to hold my head together as it felt like it was going to come apart.

"Evie!" Lark yelled and dropped down with me to the ground. He took hold of my arms and gave me a little shake as if trying to get my attention, but I couldn't look at him. My head was going to explode.

My last thought as darkness mercifully fell over me was of my child. Then, I thankfully passed out.

Chapter Eight

I found myself walking through a field heavy and thick with tall golden wheat. I remembered this place. It was then I realized I was dreaming. No. I was remembering. I was small. Maybe four years old, almost five, walking through the wheat fields pushing life into them. At four.

I was alone. No, I was not. A little tug on the belt of my white handmade cotton dress caused me to look down into the sweet face of my little brother, Lark. His hair was white gold in the morning sun. His cherub face with full cheeks stared up at me and he said in his sweet little three-year-old language, "Evie, me come too."

"K," I said back and took hold of his warm hand. Without thought or even understanding I shared with him my energy and showed him how I saw the world. I wanted him to see it as I did.

"It's a beautiful harvest, miss Eve." A woman, followed by two others, said. They were in an older version of my cotton dress. Where my golden hair hung long and free, theirs was wrapped tightly around their head. They were free of any makeup and any other personalization like jewelry or hair clips even. They were supposed to be the same in all ways. But they weren't. Even with all the sameness ordered into them, I could see them from the inside out and they were not.

The women that had called out to me, Hannah, was jealous of me. She hated me. Her two friends Ann and Maria were not much better, but the hate was contrived. Like they were told they should hate, so they did.

I pushed Lark behind me, as if a small four-year-old could protect him from three grown women. "Thank you, Hannah," I said and quickly turned and pulled Lark behind me to get back to the main farmhouse.

I found my parents there. My mother sat in a chair, being fanned by a woman, as if she were exhausted. "My special baby," she said and called out to me as if I was the only child who had walked in.

I did not go over to her. She exuded pride. Not that she had anything to do with me being special other than being a vessel. I understood that at four. The others here didn't know I was created not made. I did. I could see it in her thoughts. I could feel it in her touch. She was prideful of my gifts as they made her special in a group where everyone was supposed to be the same. It gave her power. The problem was that beneath the pride was also a little bit of fear.

My father came in behind us, strode over and yelled at Lark, "Get away from her!" He yanked Lark away from me and pushed him further aside.

My father didn't even pretend to like me. He didn't hate me. He was just further along than my mother in the fear emotions. He was afraid of me wholly and completely. I found his fear funny, as I was still a small child. He was so big to me. He felt as tall as the sky and was as strong as you could be. Yet he was afraid of me.

I get my white, blond wavy hair from him. I didn't get my eye color from anyone that I know of. I assume they are a gift from my mutation. Blue as the deep summer sky. My small frame, I get from my mother. She used that tiny size to appear weak and fragile. I hated that. She was not either of those things. She just liked the attention it got her. The same as she got from having given birth to me…the gift from God, who helped to provide them with abundance.

Lark ran back over to me and wrapped his little arms around my small body so tight you'd have thought I was trying to get away. "No," he said. Then looked up at me with his big dark eyes and said, "I can stay, right, Evie?"

I didn't get a chance to answer, as my father took hold of my brother and yanked him away again. "I said, get away from her," he snarled right in his face.

I felt such anger then, I took a step toward him and pushed my feelings of hate right back at him. I know he felt it as he flinched and dropped Lark, who fell to the ground with a cry of pain. "You need to get rid of her," he growled at my mother.

My mother turned to look at me and there was something behind her eyes I didn't understand. It was not hate, and it was not fear. Then it hit me. It was jealousy. She didn't reply to my father. She just sighed dramatically and closed her eyes as if it was all too much for her. Lark crying, my father yelling, and me just standing there watching it all.

Once she flopped down and feigned being too tired to deal, I went over to my little brother, pulled him to his feet, and took him outside with me. He stopped crying immediately. There, with his little hand in mine again, I pushed the joy of the world into him to feel. I loved my brother. He was the best part of my world in that cult. I smiled down at him as I watched him take in the beauty before him with joy.

~ * ~

I felt a cool dampness against my forehead. I pushed past the fog of sleep to awaken. Ash was at my side, and it was him pressing the cold washcloth against my head. His eyes were dark and stormy. His mouth was pinched with an emotion I didn't see often there, fear.

I reached up and touched his arm. He looked into my eyes and smiled at me. His face didn't brighten though. It still held anxiety. "Hey you. Welcome back."

"What happened? Where was I?" I asked. My brain felt foggy like I'd lost a bit of time somewhere. My voice sounded hoarse and gravely. My throat ached with the use. I was inside our home in my bed. How had I gotten there?

"That's a bit of a story," he said as he turned to lay down next to me. He wrapped me in his arms and pulled me tight against him.

"We have time," I said. "I'm not going anywhere."

"Tell me how you feel first," he asked.

I took an internal stock of my body and said, "Not bad. A little rough for some reason, but I'm good."

"How's our little nugget?" He asked.

As I'd already checked in there as well, I said, "Nugget is good too. Quiet, but just fine."

"Nora, Reed, and I were on our way back home," Ash said. "We got to about half a mile from the house and this force of air or energy, a blast of it washed over us and the car like a wave of water in the ocean. The car rocked back with it. As it came from the direction of our home, Reed stepped on the gas, and we got to you fast."

He went quiet then. I had to prod him to finish the story. "Then what?"

"Eve, it takes a lot to scare me, but what we found when we got to you, is going to give me nightmares for a month," he said and pulled me tighter to him.

"I'm sorry," I said.

He took a moment and then finished his story, "You were on your knees in the garden, the entire back yard a field of those little white flowers that keep popping up around you. Your hands were clenched against your head, and you were screaming. I've never heard you or anyone else ever make that sound. It's going to haunt me. Then to top it off, some big dude is knelt down in front of you, he has his hands on your forearms and he's calling your name, and the sound of his voice was almost as traumatic as yours. I don't even know what to tell you happened."

"I ran up to you, knocked him away from you, and the moment he let go, you stopped screaming like someone hit an off switch, and you fainted or passed out, or whatever. You fell to the ground and were still. I lifted you up and brought you in here. You were out for about an hour. I have been praying since I got you in here that you were okay."

"I don't know what to say," I said.

"I knew you were breathing calmly, and you didn't have a fever, so I have just been sitting with you, watching, and waiting for you to wake up," he said. "My God, what happened, Eve? What did that to you? Was it that guy? Cause if it was, he's a dead man."

He said it sorta like he was joking but his tone of voice said he wasn't and the fact I was skin to skin with him I could feel the turmoil within him. He was not kidding. "I don't know what happened, Ash, but that man…he's my brother. I'd forgotten him. I forgot him entirely. How is that possible?" I felt my eyes start to burn as all the memories of my little brother hit me again. His sweet self. His trusting eyes. How did I forget him?

"You have a brother? Wait? What?"

"You are just as surprised as me," I said. "I saw him at the farmer's market yesterday and he felt off. Dangerous and dark, but I couldn't figure out what it was that made me think that. I thought he was a SaneCorp goon. Then today when he touched me, all these memories and feeling gave way in my head and I couldn't…"

"Where has he been?" Ash asked quietly. He seemed as much in awe as I was.

"I don't know," I said then sat up to look at him in the face. "How could I have forgotten him, Ash? How?"

He shook his head and said, "I don't know babe. The other question is why did you forget him?"

I laid back down next to him and thought about it. "The last time I saw him, my father had contacted SaneCorp and told them they had to take me back. I don't know what all was said but the gist was I was evil, an abomination, and had to go. Lark, had me around the waist and he was screaming not to leave him. He was torn away from me, and I from him. My last memory I have is of him reaching for me, screaming my name. I was five years old. He was barely four."

I soaked in the memories that had been unleashed of my time before SaneCorp. "What does he think of me? I just left him there and never went back." Tears rolled down my face as the emotions hit me.

"Eve," Ash said.

"No, Ash. I just left him there. How could I forget him? He came looking for me. He found me. I didn't know who he was. I was afraid of him. I don't understand."

"You say he was inconsolable when you were ripped away from him. How were you?" Ash asked.

"What do you mean," I asked.

"Were you as upset as he was?"

"Yes, I was screaming and trying to get to him."

He shrugged. "Then I would guess they made you forget, or you forgot as a way to cope. Maybe it was a blessing, at the time, to give you some relief from the missing and the guilt. I'm sorrier than you know at those lost memories."

I felt myself getting hot. It was like a burst of heat shot through my entire system and I was enraged. I took a slow deep breath to try to calm down. It didn't work. It was something SaneCorp would do. It didn't even surprise me, it just enraged me.

"Eve, I don't want our room coated in little white flowers. Can you not freak out in here at least," Ash said but he was laughing. "The flowers are getting out of control."

His laughter and the fact he was right, the little green leaves and pink flowers were forming right under us in our bed, made me switch gears from anger to humor. "It's getting a bit much, right?" I asked with laughter in my own voice to match his.

"A bit," he said. "We need to figure out a way to calm that down a bit."

"Agreed," I said. Then, "So did my brother leave?"

"I actually have no idea. I grabbed you and ran."

"Ash!" I said and sat up with a start. "We need to find him. He needs to know I didn't mean to forget him!"

"Honey, take a breath. I'm sure he's still here. Granted I don't know what Nora and Reed did to him, but I'm sure they didn't let him go."

I shoved his arms off me and climbed over him to get out of the bed. "Get up. Come on, we need to go save him."

Ash took his time getting up, but he did. "I am not worried about him all that much. He looked like he could take care of himself."

"Against regular people maybe," I said and hurried to the door.

"Eve, wait for me!" Ash said with clear laughter in his voice.

I raced out of the room only to come to a startled stop, as I found Reed, sitting easily in our cushy family room chair, with Nora in his lap. Nora was animated and talking up a storm to, my brother, who sat across from them, leaning forward in clear interest and fascination at what she was saying.

"She is not as sweet as you'd think, either," Nora went on.

"No, not at all," Reed said. "She once tried to choke out a guy with a vine. That was awesome."

"Are you faking me out? I can't believe Eve would or could be mean. She is too sweet for that," Lark said.

I admit I felt a warm rush of emotion at his standing up for me even though he had not seen me in years and years, and I did in fact try to strangle that guy Reed was talking about.

As Ash came into the room with heavy steps, all the attention turned to me. That warm feeling turned into an uncomfortable blush. There was so much I wanted to say, so I was surprised when the words that came out of my mouth were, "did you know that would happen to me?"

"Hi," he said as he stood up and smiled. "You okay now?"

"Yes. So did you know?" I asked again not giving him a chance to evade the question.

"Did I think you would wig and then pass out? No. I thought something would happen, but no, that was not what I expected," he said.

He slowly came over to me and reach out to take my hand and I admit I may have flinched away pretty strongly. I saw his face fall and I felt guilty. "Sorry," I said hurriedly. "I just don't want to have that happen again. It was…a lot."

He stepped a little closer to me and said, "When we were little, you always took me outside and shared all the feelings of the world with me. The buzzing inside the plants and trees. The hum of life in the insects and animals. You shared your energy with me."

"I remember that now," I said.

"I have a theory. I could be wrong, but I think, because mom got pregnant with me so soon after you were born, there was a little bit of leftover whatever SaneCorp used to make you. I got that leftover. Then you used to share your energy with me which made me aware of what energy was and how to use it. I don't have a lot. I can't grow anything, and I can't talk to the plants and animals like you can, but I can feel the emotions of people. I can feel the life in plants and animals. The best part is I am like a human lie detector and serious empath. I have very little in the mutation department, but it's enough. I thought if I connected us again, you would feel my energy and remember me. I genuinely didn't know that explosion would happen, Eve. I'm so sorry."

I hesitated a moment partly from guilt and partly out of sadness, but then I had to know, "How did you know I had forgotten you?" My voice had shaken with emotion when I asked. I felt so bad about it. I mean how could I have forgotten a brother? How?

"Eve," Ash said and wrapped his arm around my shoulder, pulling me in against his warm body.

Lark took on a sheepish look as he glanced around the room at everyone. "Well…I remembered you and I knew I had to find you. All I ever knew was you were ripped away from me and I never saw you again. I'd ask for you all the time. Everyone would either say, later, or look at me sadly and say they were sorry. One day our great mother and father decided they didn't want to hear me cry for you anymore. So, they beat me and told me you were dead and to never ask for you again."

I cringed. I had been beaten a time or two in my small years with the cult. I knew what that was like.

"I did stop asking, but I never forgot. Every time the wheat harvest came in, I remembered walking through it with you and seeing from your eyes. It was never as bountiful after you were gone. Our parents were blamed for it." He added the last part with a big wide grin.

"When I was big enough and finally had enough of that place, I left. I went to find you. I knew you could not be dead as I felt like I would know it. We had a connection, and I still felt it. I knew if you were dead that connection would die as well. The last few years though, it's gotten stronger."

Nora turned in the chair to face us fully and said, "We've all gotten stronger the last few years. I wonder if he could feel that. All the miles and time away he still felt your energy connection. You gotta admit, Eve, that is cool as hell."

"Why didn't I feel it then?" I asked. It wasn't fair. All those years feeling so alone, and I had a brother out in the world looking for me. Yes, I had Ash and Reed and Nora now, but I'd spent years basically on my own.

"I'm getting to that," Lark said. "We didn't have much in the way of technology as you can imagine in our little family cult. Once I got out into the real world, I was fascinated by it all. I mean, it's the best thing people have made in my opinion. When you think about it, Eve, technology is a lot like you and me. It runs on energy and vibrations. Just like you and a bit like me. I have a real connection with technology. I took to it quickly and then wanted more."

That sheepish look returned. "I'm a bit of a hacker," he said and let that sentence just drop there in the room.

I don't know what he was expecting but it was not Ash's laugh and Reed's sort of harrumph.

"Another one?" Nora said. "Eve we are surrounded by these hacker dudes."

"Are all hackers the same though?" I asked. I was not a technology geek like the three guys in the room were.

"Well, yes and no," Reed said. "Some hackers are in it for the fun of the break in. Some are in it for money. Some are in it for power. Some want all three. But in the end, we are all studying code and breaking it down to break in and see what is what. So, we are the same, but we may want different things from it."

"I wanted information," Lark said as if to make sure we understood he was not in it for the money.

"I was in it for the money," Ash said. When Lark seemed a bit alarmed by that statement, he added. "Dude, I was a kid and starving. Plus, I stole from the SaneCorp. They owed me."

"I wanted all three," Reed said. "I wanted the fun of it. I wanted the money I could steal. And most importantly I wanted the information so I could take their power away from them and give it to me."

"You guys don't care I hacked into the SaneCorp systems and stole from them?" Lark asked looking a bit confused and for the first time unsure of himself.

"Nope," Reed said.

"We do it all the time," Ash added.

"Oh," Lark said. "Okay then. Well, I knew the name SaneCorp because every now and then the family unit would drop it. They'd say things like, maybe we should contact SaneCorp and ask for more money. Or you didn't get enough from that SaneCorp when you sold that girl to them. Then there was the time the family unit considered going back to SaneCorp to try to get you back as our harvest was severely poor that year and we were all hungry. It was the first time since you were born that had happened and the family unit blamed our mother and father for it. It was a bad year. Anyway, they didn't have any fear of using the name around me. They figured I didn't know what they were talking about so they could talk freely about it."

"Once I got out, I started looking into SaneCorp. Once I learned about technology I began to hack into their systems and nose about. I honestly didn't know what I was looking for but one day, I stumbled on a file about a Fugue Serum 7."

"Figures," Ash growled. "They experiment on you again with another trial drug." I felt his body heat up against me. His energy vibration became heavy.

I reached up and pulled his head down to mine and kissed him. He didn't realize it, but I used this move on him all the time. If I could change the course of his angry thoughts, to something he liked, like kissing me, his energy would usually even right back out. This wouldn't work in danger situations, but it worked in this type where his thoughts could get the better of him.

As we had enough power slippage from me in the form of little flowers everywhere, we didn't need fires added to it too. So, a simple kiss was the answer. "It was a long time ago, Ash. We can't change it now. Let's hear what he has to say."

He ran his hand from the top of my head down my back while looking me in the eyes. What was he thinking? I got the love wave, and I got the respect and awe wave. But there was always a bit of something else. I wish I could read minds totally. Especially in moments like this. "I love you," he said suddenly, uncaring of the others in the room.

"Dude," Reed said with such a tone you didn't even have to see him to know he was rolling his eyes.

"Seriously," Lark said with real disgust. "Gross."

I didn't take my eyes away from Ash, but I responded. "It's not gross. Sometimes we all just need to say it and hear it. Especially us when we never had it before." Then, to Ash I said, "I love you more."

He smiled. "Doubt it." After another long look he said. "Okay brother, let's hear the rest of it."

Lark jumped right back into his story. "I started reading about it and the more I read the more I realized what they'd done. Yes, Ash, they used it on Eve. The notes said she was inconsolable about her brother and refused to work and refused to use her gifts. She was demanding they send her home or go get me or she was not going to give them anything. She was a strong mind even then. She cried continuously. She refused to eat. They simply didn't know what to do with you. So, they gave you this Fugue Serum 7. Unfortunately for them, it didn't work the way they thought it would. You completely forgot your entire past, everything from how to walk, to how to talk, and everything about your gifts and how to use them."

"It's funny if you think about it from the research side. You had all this power just waiting to be grown and understood. When they gave the other serum, it all just vanished before their eyes, and they had to become teachers to a child. Not their forte or desire I would guess. Their research had to halt again. They hired nannies and teachers to reteach you how to do everything."

"But I did remember some of my childhood. I could not really remember my family or the family unit, but I remember being unloved, feared, and hated. I remember being beaten and abused. I remember those things, Lark."

"I'm sorry to say they most likely aren't real memories. Oh, all that stuff happened, but I bet it was memories they gave you. Think about them now as you really remember. Do they line up?"

I tried to bring up all my memories from that time of my life but now it was so crowded with new ones and foreign things that I couldn't tell what might be fake. "I don't know," I said and looked to Ash for support. "I can't tell the difference."

Ash gave me a squeeze and said, "It's okay. It's not really important. It's not."

I took a deep breath and calmed myself down. "Okay."

"Anyway, I figured out why you never came back for me. They destroyed all your memories of me so they could use you for their own purposes without the emotions I caused you."

He had been waiting for me. He hadn't said so in real words but that small slip of the tongue where he said, I never came back for him, was all I needed to hear to prove he had been waiting and hoping and wondering why I didn't.

"I'm sorry I didn't come back for you," I said. I stepped over to him and slowly and hesitantly wrapped my arms around him to give him a true but gentle hug. A part of me still wary that I would get zapped from our energy transfer again. But we didn't. Thank goodness.

"I did wait for you," he said. "I admit it. Eve, I adored you, my sister. You were everything in my life. The warm and the loving. The protector, mother, friend. You were mine. Then you were just gone, and you didn't come back. I went through periods of anger that you didn't and then sadness that you didn't and even periods wondering why. Were you mad at me? What could keep you away."

"Honestly, finding that report on the Fugue Serum 7, was the best thing that I could have found because it gave me the understanding that no, you did not forget me. They forcefully removed you from me in all ways. Personally, removed you from my side and then ripped me out of your mind. You didn't forget me. That was all I needed to know."

I felt the cool wetness as tears rolled down my face. His words broke my heart and at the same time made me feel loved. "I'm still so sorry. Especially cause even when you were right in front of my face, I didn't see it. I felt something off and I felt fear because of it. It took you forcing my hand to make me see. Hey," I said a thought occurring to me. "How did you know you had to touch me? To make me remember? How did you know?"

"There was a small side note at the bottom of the article on you. It said the boy and specimen A had a bond that was more than only emotional and if that bond were to be rejoined it could undo Serum 7. I was to be kept away from you entirely to make sure that did not happen. It took me some time to figure that one out. I knew I was the boy, and you were specimen A, but rejoining a bond was a little strange for me."

"Smart," Reed said. "I like him."

He chuckled. "Not too smart, I tried just getting her to see me first and thinking that would do it. When that had no change in her I spent some time thinking about it. When we were little, we used to walk through the farm fields. You remember, Eve? You would hold my hand and share your energy powers with me. I didn't know that was what she was doing, only that when she held my hand, I could see more and feel more of the world around me."

"I remember," I said. "I just dreamed about it, and now I remember it all. The feel of your warm small hand and me pushing my power into you just enough so you could see the world the way I did. We didn't have anyone else. You were my everything. I wanted you to see my world too."

"I was still a little in shock at seeing you up close and personal for the first time since we were small. You were this ethereal beauty with white golden hair and these bright blue eyes. You are lovely. You are just as I would have thought, but better."

"There is something pure and sweet about her isn't there," Ash asked. "It's all fake. She's a spicy one."

Nora burst out laughing and Reed lifted one small corner of his mouth to show his own enjoyment of Ash's way untrue statement. "Whatever!" Nora said. "She is exactly as she appears. That's one of her bad traits if you ask me."

"Me being nice is a bad thing?" I asked.

"Yes, you let people hurt you and take advantage of you, and you put up with a bunch of shit that would not have ever happened had you just been a bitch in the first place."

Ash tilted his head and gave me a snarky grin. "She's not wrong. I will say, the last few months I've seen a different view. You have to admit it too, Nora. She has a temper. I was surprised to find out.

"You could set anyone's teeth on edge," Reed said completely deadpan.

Ash flipped him off but didn't respond otherwise. Lark laughed obviously enjoying the family type banter. We all picked at one another, but I knew there was love there. Even from Reed. He may seem grumpy, but he was an old softy. I saw him. He was gentle with me. He loved his Nora. Oh yeah, he was a marshmallow. He held a lot of emotions inside him though. I felt them and saw them, it was why I loved him too.

"So," Lark said breaking back in, "I used that memory of Eve and thought maybe a touch. Her connecting with my energy and me connecting with hers would open a door in her mind."

"It did that," I said remembering the rush of memories gushing in. The noise of them crashing through my brain was horrendous. What was worse was that I felt the emotions of the memories too, and that was painful.

I didn't know about the wave of energy we sent out into the world, but I felt the connection between Lark and me rejoin and it almost did me in.

"Now what?" Nora asked.

"What do you mean?" I asked.

"What do we do with your brother?" Reed answered.

"He stays with me," I said or more like stated firmly. He was not going anywhere. He was not leaving me, ever again.

"That's not what I meant," Reed said with this tone that set my teeth on edge. What was it…placating. That was the world.

"We aren't saying he has to go, Eve. We just meant, what now?" Ash added but he also had a tone.

What the hell, I felt my temperature rise. I was missing something. I looked to Nora for some indication, and she just pointed to the floor. I didn't even have to look down to know. "Damnit!" I said. "Why?"

Lark looked at the group and said, "Am I missing something?"

"I am having some sort of emotional power leakage," I said harshly. It was directed at myself and not anyone else. I took a deep breath then pulled the energy I had used to grow the little crop of pink flowers at my feet, away from them. They withered and died and then turned to ash. "I gotta stop doing that."

Lark shrugged and said, "I think it's cool."

"Well, it is, and it isn't," Nora said. "It's cool, in that she can do it with her mind, but it's not as she's not in control and it can cause others, normal people to see it and wonder and that puts us in a bad situation. We have enough to contend with, with only SaneCorp coming for us. Think about how bad it could be if other research and weapons companies knew about us? We'd never be free."

We all went silent. Each one of us thinking our own thoughts of doom, I'm sure. "Lark can stay in the spare room, I guess. Or the couch."

"Couch city is fine by me," he said and grinned.

"We travel light. How much crap do you have with you?"

I laughed. I already knew that answer.

Lark smiled too. "I travel light too. We were never allowed possessions growing up. I have only a few personal clothing items and personal care stuff. That's it."

"Cool," Reed said. "Like I said, smart."

"I'll help you get settled then," Ash said.

"I can help," I said.

Lark shook his head. "Sorry, Eve. I think Ash and I need to talk. I have things to say, and I think he does too."

"How do you know what I have to say," Ash asked a little wary.

After the last guy tried to read our minds, we were all a little wary to be honest.

"Empath…remember?" Lark said and stood up. "My bag is outside."

They both turned to head out the door. "Ash," I said stopping him before he was out of sight.

He turned, walked back over to me. He cupped my face and gently placed a kiss on my waiting lips. "Don't worry babe. I got this."

"I know. Don't run him off, please," I said.

He gave me a quick salute and walked out the door. I left them to it. While I waited, I went to the little closet by the door and pulled out the old and barely functional sweeper and ran it around the house. The daisy ashes everywhere were getting out of hand.

I felt a small warmth inside my tummy low and barely there, but I felt it. My little nugget agreed with me I decided. We had to figure this flower thing out.

Chapter Nine

It was decided I should have someone with me at the farmer's market. Nora worked with people at the pizza shop and Reed and Ash also had co-workers with them. I was the only one basically on my own. Yes, there were other vendors at the market, but we didn't feel they would look after me the same as co-workers in case there were issues. Maybe Connie would…but that was the only one that I thought of an actual friend in the making. Or at least a work friend.

With that decided, Lark was my new market partner in crime. I loved this idea. One, it would give me a chance to get to know my brother again. All I had were memories from when we were children. We had been apart for a long time. Almost fifteen years.

This also worked in a practical sense in that now the others didn't have to take turns helping me load, set-up, break down, and re-load each market day. It was a good solution for all of us.

The following day was a market day, so Lark and I were on it. Nora caught a ride into town with us as she had a shift. "I'll be sure to bring home dinner tonight. If you have any requests, text me," she said as we were heading out the door.

Reed and Ash did not have to work, so they were going to stay home and do some research on where the SaneCorp facilities were located.

By the time we got to our spot and set up, the market was open and hopping. We didn't have much chance to chit chat other than basic directional things like, where do you want these, or can you pull that down?

Once we fell into a decent grove, and after the silence got too awkward, I finally opened the conversation and said, "tell me about your life. How was it growing up in the cult after I left?"

I asked it with a smile as although we'd never called ourselves a cult, as adults and looking back, that is exactly what it was.

"Not much changed after you left. There were more people who joined over the years, and some also left during that time too. Our harvests were never the same though after you were gone."

I didn't interrupt. I just let him talk as we worked.

"Mom was more upset than you would expect. She lost a lot of attention and actually had to start doing her share of the chores. Then when the harvests started to be a problem, she wanted to bring you back. You were after all a gift from God and how could everyone have shunned this gift!" He chuckled here. "As if she wasn't one of the people who helped to get rid of you. But dear ole dad put a stop to that real quick. Once I got older, I realized he was afraid of you. Not just a little nervous but full heart stuttering, sweat inducing, scared of you. I admit to getting a bit of joy out of that."

"Glad to hear it as then I'm not the only one," I said and laughed. "He was a real piece of work."

"It's a little funny," he said, "for a time after you were gone, he was nicer, easier. That didn't last as life became harder as food became less and work became more. Plus, with more people, there came more babies, and as we continued to grow, the food situation grew worse. He took the blame for most of that, especially in the eyes of the ones that had been there when you were still around. They knew he was the reason the crops were less, and food was less, and money was less. They weren't subtle about it either."

"They got louder about it too, saying things like, Eve would have taken care of this easy. Or we never had this problem when Eve was here. Sometimes it was just wishing and memories, like you should have seen the harvest when Eve was around. He would come home mad and stay mad. I used to go outside the moment he came inside and stayed away until it was time for bed. I rarely ate dinner with the family. It was easier to just be unseen."

"Didn't you have any good times?" I asked. The idea the last fifteen plus years of his life were miserable, was not a thought I liked.

"I did actually," he said. "A family joined who had several kids. One was my age. Her name was Amanda."

"Ooo young love," I said all soft and dreamy.

"It was," he said, but then he was quiet for a moment.

I stopped moving zucchini from a crate to the table to look at him. I felt an overwhelming sadness suddenly come off him. "What happened?"

"I wish I could say it was just a childhood crush and a broken heart," he said. After a moment he continued, "She got sick. Didn't get better."

That was a very simple and direct way of saying she died. I took a breath to calm my instant need to fix an unfixable situation or to take the blame which had I been there I might have been able to help. Instead of all that I just took his hand and said, "I'm so sorry."

He looked me in the eye and said, "Me too."

I went back to zucchini sorting, and he went back to helping customers. After a little while he said, "I left soon after. I couldn't stay there anymore."

I completely understood that. I decided to change the topic. I wanted to know more about Amanda, but I didn't think it was the time for that. We were newly reacquainted, and I didn't want to close him off with deep discussions. "Did we get any more brothers or sisters?"

"Thank God, no!" He said emphatically and with a heavy dose of disgust. "They never should have had any children, so I'm insanely grateful they didn't have anymore."

"They weren't the best of parents, but I don't like the idea of you being alone," I said.

"I wasn't. We had a lot of kids in the group. When you were there, I always just stuck to you. Once you were gone, I had to branch out, otherwise I would have been alone. It wasn't all bad, Eve. Some of it was terrible, you know how it was. The beatings and the abuse and after you were gone the hunger and the neglect, but there were good things too. I promise I won't lie to you. Not about this or anything."

"I won't either," I said and held out my hand. He took it and we did a sort of little shake as if to bind our agreement. I smiled at him and said, "Deal!"

That night when we got home, I felt happier. I had not realized I was unhappy until I wasn't anymore. Having Lark with me throughout the day, sharing our lives and our thoughts and just picking up from where we left off made me happy.

We still had so much to catch up on, but we made a good start. If we could just start to not feel so awkward around each other that would be awesome.

When Ash met us at the car, gave me my welcome home kiss, and asked the usual question of "How was your day?" I had a real answer.

"It was a good day!"

"It really was, too," Lark said.

"How was your day?" I asked back.

"We got a good media plan ready to go. As soon as Nora gets back with dinner, we can chat about it."

As if she knew we were talking about her, Nora arrived. A co-worker had brought her home, as we were right on their way. Or so she said. Either way, it was good timing. "Hey," she said as she rolled out of the little white and rusted car.

"Awesome timing! I'm starving," Ash said as he took all the boxes and bags from her to carry inside.

Once we were all sorted and settled on chairs, couches, and even the floor for Lark, Reed told us what he had found.

"Okay, so it looks like there are four main campuses left for SaneCorp. New York, Alabama, Idaho, and New Mexico." We have done a search on all the media sources we could find in a hundred-mile radius of these sites, and we have a package ready to go out to them with our evidence of…I'm actually not even certain what to call it."

"Foul play?" Nora said.

"Fraud? Negligence?" Ash added.

"Murder," I said.

"Well, yes and no. All of that, but we don't have evidence of murder so far. Just the possibility of it. But…" he continued on before anyone could interrupt him. I say anyone but I mean me. "We will give them all the evidence we have and let them figure it out on their own. Ash and I talked and thought if they have to do research into it, they may feel more connected to it. If they feel a connection, they will work harder to prove it. Ya know?"

I agreed with that.

"Okay. When does the package go out?" Nora asked.

"It's ready now. We can send it whenever we want," Ash said.

"Tomorrow is good for me," Lark added in. "I know I don't have as much history as you all but I'm in this with you. I think the sooner we get this started, the sooner we are free of them."

"So, the packages go out tomorrow then," Reed said.

I put my hand over the tiny bump of life sitting quietly in my body. I sent out a little whisper to it. A sort of, are we ready?

My little nugget didn't respond in words or thought. It was just too small. I did get a flush of warmth though. It wasn't a yes, we are ready or a no we are not. It was just a *I'm here and I'm with you* sort of feeling. I guess ready or not, we were going to do it.

The media packages went out as scheduled.

The days and nights went forward as usual.

We were all on our guard, waiting for the results of our actions. Whenever any of us went to town, the rest of us waited for them to come back with any news. There was no news and no news for days and then a week went by. There was no news story that we saw. And we looked for one. The guys were always checking the internet and the news stations and the media sites for any breaking news or even a story on the issue. There was just nothing.

Lark and I were at the market a few weeks later. It was full on summer at this point, and I made sure to have plenty of veggies and fruits available. I had many regulars who came at least once a week for their produce shop. Ours was the go-to stand for any produce you wanted. If I could just talk the others into a few chickens and maybe a goat or two, we could add eggs and goat cheese and milk. So far though, none of the others were up for it.

I would wait them out though. Sooner or later, we'd get them. One of their arguments was we didn't know how long we would be able to stay there. We might end up having to leave. Leaving behind plants was one thing, leaving animals was another.

I did agree with them, but I wanted to plan for the future. It's hard to do that when you can't put down any roots.

"So, you see the dog food stand? One down and across the aisle?" I said quietly to Lark as I set out the peaches, I had ready. They were out of season for many people, but not for me. I figured I could pull off one or two more weeks of peaches before people started questioning how I had them.

Lark stopped organizing the boxes behind me to look down the aisle. "Yeah," he said and went back to work.

"See the lady directly next to him?"

"Yeah," he said.

"They are having an affair," I said.

Lark turned to face me directly and said, "Nuh uh! How do you know?"

I laughed and said, "Anyone could tell if they looked, but they are also putting off enough lovesick energy it's actually making me a little nauseous."

"But aren't they both married?"

"Yup. And in case you are wondering, not to each other. The dog guy has a sweet wife, named Kari, and they have two kids, both girls. The bow lady has a husband but no children."

"Ew," he said.

"Yeah. It doesn't matter if you are born in a cult or just a regular person, the human animal is selfish."

"What are you going to do about it?"

I laughed and said, "Not a thing. It's none of my business."

"But you know," he said.

I shrugged and said "I know they have a thing. I know they are both married. That's it. There is a lot more to affairs than that. Heck for all I know they are in open marriages."

He looked from the guy to the girl and said, "You think?"

I shrugged again and said, "Look how we were raised? It was one big open marriage."

"True."

I started to laugh until I felt red angry energy flow over me from behind. I snapped up poker straight, as sudden, and real fear matching the red emotion swirling around me exploded inside me. "Lark?"

He noticed my change immediately and stepped close. "What it is? Where?"

"It's behind me. Not close, but close enough I can feel them. Can you look over my shoulder and see anything? Anyone?"

"I don't see anything," he said. He glanced down at his watch and said, it's almost time to head home. Is Nora catching a ride with us?"

"Yea, you should go find her. Make sure she gets to us safely," I said.

"I'm not leaving you," he said.

"Look. I'm surrounded by people. If it's SaneCorp, they are looking for me or Nora. I don't think they are looking for you. Go meet her on her walk over and just stick to her. I'm fine here. Just…hurry."

He seemed to be having a small argument in his head, but finally he said, "Okay. Don't go anywhere and don't lift anything. Little nugget is growing in there. I'll be back to lift and carry."

I smiled as he used my term 'nugget' for the baby. "I won't."

"I mean it," he said again.

"I mean it too. I won't. Promise."

"Okay," he said and turned on his heel and went in search of Nora. I sent a wave to Connie, who smiled and waved back. I let myself feel the energy of the people around me. Even the dog food guy and the bow lady. Everyone felt normal. Some happier than others. Some sad or frustrated. The only red energy I felt was from the one area of question behind me at the edge of the market.

Not close, but not far either. I had felt okay sending Lark out to find Nora, so she didn't have to walk alone here. However, I felt his absence more than I thought I would. The sooner they made it back the better I would feel that's for sure.

I kept my eyes peeled for them while also watching for a stranger or strangers. I know I didn't recognize every single person who visited the market each day, but very few came over to my stall with rage riding under the skin.

It only took about twenty minutes for me to see Lark and Nora striding toward me. The relief I felt was like a weight lifted from my shoulders. There was nothing wrong and yet, I knew the bad was coming. I didn't know how or really from what direction, but it was coming for us.

Spark

We packed up as usual without any incident or sightings of anything to be concerned about. We loaded the car, and we headed out. My head was swinging back and forth watching, looking, and trying to see the bad that was looming out there where I couldn't see it. Lark and Nora, I saw were doing the same.

We made it out of town and still nothing. We made it out to the back road, and nothing was there. Then, out of nowhere, a tan car, came up behind us, fast. I felt the energy of them before I saw the car, so I'd turned around to look out the back window.

In what I believed would be a very calm voice, I said, "They are going to hit us."

As the words left my mouth though, I'm sorry to say, I was not calm, and my voice was not easy. I was shouting. Nora turned around from the passenger seat to look. Lark just glanced in the rear-view mirror.

The car came at us fast and rammed us once. Our car rocked on its axle and weaved a moment before Lark was able to get it back under control. He sped up and said, "Hang on, ladies. We may be in for a ride."

He said it as a sort of joke, but I didn't find it funny. I was too afraid.

I didn't give any notice to the others. I just pushed my powers outward and called the plants to help. Vines from the ditches next to the road, poured out over the berm and onto the blacktop. They stretched out their long thick vines, grabbed hold of and wrapped around the wheels and the frame of the tan sedan.

Unfortunately, the vines were breaking and snapping away as fast as they could take hold. They were not stopping the car, but they were slowing it down. I reached for more and more plants to come to our aid. I decided to put all the strength I could into one side of the car. If I could pull it off balance, it might set them out of control.

Inside the car, I suddenly felt cold. The windows began to fog over. Then frost began to form around the edges of the windows. Nora had taken up the battle with me and I saw ice begin to form in what looked like tire tracks under the car. She was pushing the ice from the floor of the interior of the car to the road underneath.

With my vines pulling to one side, added to the now very icy road conditions behind us, the tan sedan didn't stand a chance. It rocked to the right against the berm. I watched as it swerved and careened to the left. Then it hit the small lip where berm changes to green space and I knew it was over. The car jolted and then flipped, going airborne as it turned over once, then twice, before it crashed to the ground with the wheels up in the air, still slowly spinning. Smoke floated upward from the hood, and a small spot under the carriage of the car.

Larked had slowed down to watch the crash, but once it landed, we continued on toward home. I turned back around in my seat and settled back in comfortably.

I suppose some would ask, how do you know they were bad people? They felt bad. Plus do good people come up behind you and ram you while you are driving? Then rear back, rev up and come at you to do it again? I don't think so.

Was I upset or guilty feeling for leaving them there to their fate? Nope. I had my own little family to worry about.

We made it home safe and sound after that. As we got out, Ash and Reed met us at the car. They took one look at the dented and crunched backend and chaos reigned for a few minutes.

Everyone was talking and shouting and asking questions. I expected no less. "Hey, we are all okay. Nora and I worked together to take them out. Lark took care of driving like a mad boss and kept us safe while we did."

Reed threw his hands up in the air and said, "Why did I even bother getting you all phones? Not one of you called to warn us or even sent a hey we had a little trouble text. What the hell?"

"We were almost home," I said thinking that was a good answer.

"You remember that if I am ever out and have a run in and don't call or let you know. I will be sure to tell you later when I'm home," Ash said with a very hard tone. One I don't know that I had ever heard, or at least not ever directed at me.

But he was also somewhat right. I would be very mad if he didn't call me. We were almost home though. It was like five minutes from the crash home. I can't say about the others, but I'd used that time to process what had happened. Had we been further from home, I was sure I would have let him know.

"Hey," I said. "That's not fair. We didn't intentionally set out to upset you or keep you in the dark. That's not what we are going to be doing. I'm sorry you are upset. I will do better if there is a next time."

"I'm sorry too," Nora said. "I didn't think five minutes would matter, but from the other side, I would be upset."

"I was driving," Lark said with humor. "Couldn't text and drive man."

I quickly jumped in front of Lark and playfully said to Nora, "Don't hit him! He doesn't know any better."

That was all we needed. A little comic relief to a tense situation. "At least we know someone is doing something with our media packages," I said.

We had only been standing out there a few minutes when we heard the sound of sirens in the distance.

"Is that the cops?" Nora asked, her eyes wide. "That seems a little fast, don't you think?"

"Should we hide the car," Lark asked. He didn't seem all that perturbed with the idea of the cops zooming in on us. He also hadn't been on the run for most of his life.

Reed thought a second and said, "Nope. We are going to call them ourselves."

"What!" I shouted. "Why would we do that!"

"Eve. Flowers," Ash said and pointed at my feet.

"Damnit!" I shouted again as the little spring daisy flowers popped out under me.

Before we could stop him, Reed pulled out his phone and called emergency services. "Yes, we've had an incident. Can you send an officer out? Yeah, some guy tried to run us off the road."

He gave them our address and few more yeahs, then hung up. I stared at him dumbfounded. "Why?" I asked.

"Look you guys, they were already on the way. Normal people, when faced with some car ramming into them and chasing them down the street, call the police. It would look bad for us if we didn't."

Ash nodded his head and said, "He's right. Let's get our story straight."

98

~ * ~

"And then, they went off to the side of the berm and it was like they got tangled up on the weeds and lost control," Nora told the police officer who had introduced himself of Officer Allen.

"Why didn't you stop when the accident happened?" He asked.

"It was just me and another girl in the car. What were we going to do? Plus, the guy had tried to kill us. We didn't have a phone on us, and we were almost home. I booked it to the house and told Reed what happened. He called you guys right away."

The second officer on the scene was Officer Davis. He chimed in, and asked Eve, "Is that an accurate telling?"

I was trying really hard to make sure all my energy and forces were buttoned up tight so there were no sudden flowers arriving around us. I was glad Nora had taken the lead on the interrogation. "Yes. I think that's about it. Honestly, I was so scared I don't know what would have happened had I been driving. I was pretty much just screaming. I am not even sure what happened. Why did they do that? What could we have possibly done to them?"

Then I turned on the best acting you have ever seen in your life and started to cry. Since my emotions were already super close to the surface, I just let them run free and sobbed openly and freely. Then I leaned into Officer Davis and made him incredibly uncomfortably while crying all over him.

As I was now touching him, I was able to press a little bit of emotional energy into Officer Davis. Just a bit of sympathy and caring. Emotional energy is a fun perk that I have thanks to my gift. I didn't have the opportunity to use very often, but when I did, it came very naturally to me.

Plus, the crying on my end wasn't all acting. It had been scary. They hadn't been trying to get to us. They had been trying to kill us. That was new.

"Eve honey," Ash said as he transferred my emotional self from Officer Davis to his shoulder and walked me a few feet away from him.

"There is no rhyme or reason for evil. He was probably just picking a car at random and set out to scare you. It's okay."

"Well, I think we have all the information we need here," Officer Davis said.

"Actually, I have one more question," Officer Allen said. "How do you know it was one guy in the car."

Reed shrugged and said, "We don't. The girls told us what happened, and I just assumed it was a guy. Why? Was it not?"

"No further questions. We will be in touch." Officer Allen snapped closed his little notebook and the two officers got into their car and headed out. Just like that.

"They didn't tell us not to leave town," Nora said sarcastically.

"Did that go as you thought it would," Lark said as he came out from where he was quietly hiding in the house. We'd decided the less people involved the better. Plus, the people in town knew us. Sorta. Lark was a stranger as he's only been in town a few weeks.

"Yeah. They wanted to be all big and bad and act threatening but because we stuck together and to our story, it didn't really work. Plus, Eve, that was a stroke of genius blubbering all over the man. There was nothing they could really do to us. We gave them our version of what happened. Had no idea of the why or the who so they couldn't really do anything with it."

"Plus keeping it just the two girls in the car, they seemed to go easy on them. I doubt that if they knew Lark was in the car with them, they would have. I have a feeling they would have tried to tear him apart for information. Eve crying made them nervous, so they headed out."

I knew I had the look of sweet innocence, but what it also meant was I looked weak. Men with strength or thought they had any power, liked to think I needed taking care of and handled. I used their ignorance against them. If they wanted to think I was dumb and weak, that is all they would get out of me.

"That's why I love Ash. He knows I may be sweet looking, but I am far from weak and innocent."

"Oh man you should have seen her with those vines too. They just came up out of the ditch like something out of the movies. Dirt was flying up like a geyser and these big thick arm-like branches reached out and grabbed their car and shook it around like a rag doll. She didn't hesitate. She just took action. That was awesome, Eve. I don't think I told you that," Nora said.

"Yeah, Nora is right. I was too busy trying to stay on the road and ahead of them. I was on the defense. Eve and Nora both went right to the offense and attacked. They were so cool."

"I don't get your sports reference. You know that right?" I said feeling very self-conscious. They were all staring at me.

"Yeah, I know. You got the gist though," Lark said.

"So, do you think they bought our story? Do you think they will come back?" I asked.

Reed shrugged and Ash did the same, but he said. "I guess we will find out. Just stick to the story and we should be fine."

"Speaking of not leaving town," Reed said as we all trudged into the house, "I think our next steps, outside of our next series of media mailings, is to start visiting the last four buildings. See what we can find."

"Visit? Or break in?" Nora asked with a grin. "Either is fine by me."

Reed and Ash just grinned back. Yeah, we all understood what Reed meant.

"I'm coming too," Lark stated. He didn't ask. He stated.

"About that," Reed said. "I think maybe just a couple of us should go."

"No," I and Nora said at almost the same time.

"We are stronger together. We learned that the hard way, but we learned it. If one goes, we all go. Period," I said.

"Exactly," Nora said. "No one goes alone. We all go, or no one goes."

Reed looked at Ash, who rolled his eyes. "Eve, maybe now is not the time for you to be out, fighting evil in the world."

"Who do you think they will be coming for first, Ash?" I asked. My hands were on my hips, and I found myself standing directly in front of him. He was my focus as he was mine and he mattered more than the rest. If he was on my side, I wouldn't have to fight the others. "That's right, me! I have the most to lose as I'm carrying the next generation of biological meta humans. They will come for me and our baby. If I'm here on my own, how strong am I? If I am with you, we are strong together. I am safer and stronger, and baby is safer."

Ash looked just at me. He closed off from the others as I did. It was like we were having a private conversation.

"You know I'm right," I said when I felt him waver.

Ash sighed and nodded once at me. He said more for the benefit of the others, "She's right, you guys. We are stronger as a group. We can't separate, especially as we are picking a fight. They will respond like they did today. We should stay together."

Nora and Reed didn't put up any fight. Nora just said, "Okay."

Reed took it a step further and said, "Well then we need to start making plans."

"Wait," Lark said. "You can't be serious? She's pregnant. You can't let her be in danger like that."

Ash started to respond but I stepped forward and spoke to Lark instead. "Lark, no one lets any of us do anything. No one is the boss of the other. No one makes rules for the others. We all have an equal say in the group, and we have full say in our own lives."

"Eve, what if you get hurt?" Lark said.

"Lark, you know a little about what it's like to be trapped and feel like a prisoner. You were able to leave the farm when you were old enough. No one came after you. No one stopped you. We didn't have that. We had to escape and then we had them coming for us at every turn. We felt hunted. We have been hunted. No one gets to decide what I can and can't do anymore. Not even you. I love you all, but I am my own boss. We all are in control of our own lives. That's it."

"I'm scared of losing you. Again," he said quietly.

I wrapped my arms around him and hugged him tightly. "If we work together and stay together, no one will lose anyone. We are a team."

He hugged me tight to him in response. "Okay. I will keep that in mind, but that doesn't mean I'm not going to worry about you and likely make you a little insane over it."

I laughed and so did Ash. "I have no doubt," I said.

"No worries, dude. She will make you just as insane. Take it from the ones who know," Ash said.

Reed and Nora both chimed in with their own form of agreement.

With that settled we got busy putting our plans into action. It was decided we would hit Georgia first. It was heavy summer and that would have been an issue for Nora if we went west, but as Georgia was more humid, she should be able to handle the heat with the water in the air to pull from.

From there we would head out to New Mexico. We did have concerns about that area. One because I had history there. I'd lived there for years in my own little sanctuary. But it was also a dry hot that would affect Nora. We had to take extras steps to make sure she would be okay. We'd have plenty of water and a good car with strong AC for when she needed it.

After we hit those two stops, we'd come home to go through and discuss what to do next. It would depend on what we found out. If we found nothing, we would know what to expect. If we found evidence, real concrete evidence, then we would have to decide what to do with it.

It was settled. We would head out as soon as we could get the trip planned.

With that in mind, at the farmer's market on Wednesday, I hunted down Connie. I would have to close the garden while we were gone. Not really close it down, like a regular person would, but close my part of it. Basically, put things into regular processing and growing patterns. We'd be gone about a week or so. That meant, I needed to get someone to water the plants, so it seemed normal.

"Sure!" Where are you all going? I hope it's someplace fun," Connie said.

I had not expected her to ask questions, which was dumb on my part. I had to think on my feet, "We are heading south. Going on a road trip to the gulf. Who knows where we will end up, but we needed a break from the every day."

"Oh, I get it. I keep saying I should get out of here for a bit too. When do you guys leave?" She asked.

"Saturday," I said. If you come one day on the market off day, I can show you around the garden. Give you an idea of what it will need while I'm gone."

"I can come tomorrow. You can show me around your digs!"

That was easy enough. With my garden sorted, all I needed to do was pack.

We left town bright and early on Saturday morning as expected. We were not on a time frame, but we did want to get an early start to make it as far south as we could. We had not had any more visits from anyone we believed to be from SaneCorp in the days leading up to our trip. We also had not heard anything more from the police on the incident.

Chapter Ten

We stopped at the minimart gas station just after leaving town behind. We filled our arms with drinks and snacks, along with the car full of gas, then we were on our way. It was a minimum of a twelve-hour drive to the first of our stops in Georgia.

If we drove hard with little stops, we could do it in a day, but thanks to my bladder and having to stop every two hours, we had to make one stop the first night but made it there the next day by mid-morning.

I rolled myself out of the car and said, "I have never been so glad to be out of a car in my life."

"That back seat felt small today," Ash said as he unfolded himself from the car after me.

I needed a restroom, again, and I was hungry. "Let's find a place to eat and make a plan of action," I said.

Reed looked at his phone to check the time and said, "I could eat."

There was a little greasy diner called Ma's across the street. We were happy to walk over to it, after being stuck in the car all day. We slid into a booth towards the back, and settled in. After the restroom was visited, and our orders were placed, we got down to business.

"We are about twenty-six miles from what I think is a warehouse. After we finish here, we can find a hotel for the night. Then after dark, we can go check out the place."

I turned to Nora and Ash and said, "You guys have all the stuff you need to get us inside?" Meaning the tools of a thief.

Ash squeezed me against him and said, "Don't need much. A little heat, a bit of know-how, and a little muscle, I can get us in."

Nora rolled her eyes and said, "We can get us in."

Ash shrugged and said, "Okay, we can get in. Either way, we got this."

"I think we should talk about what to do with what we find," Reed said.

"I have no idea what is in there, we can't plan for what we don't know," Ash responded.

"I agree," Nora said. "We will have to play it by ear. Wing it. There could be nothing there or there could be a lot. If it's just data, make sure to have plenty of space on your portable drive to collect it. Other than that, we will just have to see what we find."

"Eve?" Reed asked. "Any thoughts from you on this?"

"I was just thinking I should have brought one of the wolves with us. If I had time, I bet I could train them to be guardians and to help us sniff out things," I said.

"A bit off topic," Reed said.

"I know, but you asked if I had any thoughts. Those were my thoughts. Aside from that, I agree with the others. We can't plan for what we don't know."

"We can plan a bit. We know to bring a drive with a lot of space. We know we have to bring the tool kits to get us in. You are going to be our alarm system, Eve. You can do all the things your wolves can, and quieter."

He was not wrong. I just didn't trust that part of me yet. It felt too new. I had only been practicing with that for a short period of time. In comparison to my main gifts anyway. The creating life part. "Okay. I'll do my best," I said, and I meant it.

"We all have faith in you, babe," Ash said.

Our food finally arrived, and after scarfing it down, we put our plans into action. We found a hotel about ten miles out from the warehouse. We checked in, and I took a nap. It wasn't that I did all that much, as we'd been in the car for two days. But being in the car for two days seemed to be exhausting, for me at least.

Night fell and we headed out toward our destination. We parked the car off the road in the ditch when we were within half a mile of the place.

"De ja-vu," I said.

"My thoughts exactly," Nora said.

The warehouse was a carbon copy of the building we had just torched a few months back. It sat in a fallow field. The building was grey and white, and it rose out of the nothingness of that field into a giant four-story building of stone. It was lit up so brightly, the halo of the light was able to be seen from a distance of half a mile away.

"How do you want to do this?" Lark asked.

"Yeah, we know there are cameras all over the place," Ash added.

"We need to get in behind them. Then Ash can do his thing," Reed said.

"What's his thing?" Lark asked.

"He can either melt them so they don't work, smoke the glass so they can't see anything, or get in from the back of them and just turn them off," I said.

"Really?" He asked quite impressed.

"Yeah," Ash said. "Depends on my mood as well as where the camera is sitting and how easy it is to get to the back." He then grinned at us all and said, "Or how much fun I feel like having."

I giggled. "Let's stay with easiest, quietest and best so we don't get caught at the first warehouse. We have three more to get to."

"Okay gang let's go. Slow and low to the ground," Reed said and crouched down. He moved easily through the low weeds of what I could tell was once a wheat field. The wheat was dead, but the stalks were still up off the ground about two feet. Not a lot, but enough to use to our advantage.

He moved on silent feet, and slow motions, and before I knew it, he was out of my sight. Nora followed behind him, and then Lark, and then Ash.

"Let's do this," Ash said with a smile before turning and dropping low and moving into the line of the others.

"Right behind you," I said. As soon as he was a little way in front to me, so as not to crowd him, I also crouched down low to the ground and realized with a bit of chagrin that my stance was not comfortable. My tummy was not all that big, and I was hardly showing my little nugget, but it was full, and it felt hard. Plus, there was not a lot of space for my insides to adjust as I was bent down into such a low squat. "Oh, this is going to suck," I said for my own benefit.

I took in an uncomfortably breath and slowly went in behind the others. My headway was slow because I couldn't get in a good breath. My lungs felt constricted and any air I got in felt shallow and as if it was not enough.

I kept going though, and thankfully about twenty minutes later, I came to a stop just on the edge inside the field where the others had stopped. I immediately laid down flat on my back and took in a full breath, while I allowed my organs to go back where they wanted.

"What took you so long?" Ash whisper yelled at me. "I was about ready to come back for you."

I didn't say a word, I just patted my tummy. They could make of that what they wanted. I wasn't in the mood to explain it.

Reed frowned at me but didn't say a word. Ash did take my hand and ask, "You good?"

I just nodded. I was fine now. Ready to rock.

Reed pantomimed all sorts of motions, but I didn't understand a one of them. I thought he was saying we would go around the side and walk up to the front, but then he may have said we were going around the front and walk right in. "Dude…they have cameras, not mics."

His face turned to steel, and he whispered into our group, "We don't know what they have!"

"Well, it's better to have us all on the same page than trying to guess what the plan is," Ash agreed.

"Fine," Reed said.

Nora took his hand and placed it over her heart. She didn't say anything, just gave him a small smile. I was not certain they couldn't talk inside each other's head. They did that a lot. Just sorta communicated without words. It was sweet and sometimes a little annoying if I was honest. Then again everything annoyed me easily lately, so what did I really know?

I watched as Reed took a long and slow breath and let it out just as slowly. Then he said, "Okay, we are going to go around the back. Eve, we know there are windows up there, I want to see if we can just go in one of the higher windows. It may not be locked up there."

"They always locked our windows?" Ash said.

"That was because we were there. They were locking us in more than keep anything out," Nora said.

"True," Ash said.

"So, you want me to create a way up," I said understanding right away what they were thinking. Less cameras out back and up high. It was a good plan.

They all began a little crab-like walk to the back of the building. Me, I was not doing that again. I got down on my hands and knees and just crawled this time. It was faster and not as uncomfortable.

Ash lifted an eyebrow at me but didn't say a word. We came in almost dead center to the building and leaned up against the walls while everyone surveyed our surroundings.

Ash pointed to one of the corners. I followed his direction and saw one camera near the roof edge. I turned my head and checked the other corner wall and sure enough there was another one. We all then tried to see the rest of the back, but I didn't see any other cameras.

Evidently the others didn't either as Reed crawled over to my side and asked, "So. What are you thinking to get us up to those top windows?"

I needed something quick, so a tree was not really going to cut it. I could do a vine quick and easy, but I didn't think everyone would want to do that type of climb, including me. I stepped up over close to the building under where a big window was about two stories high.

I concentrated and pulled energy from around me and pushed it into the ground, where two vines instantly began to grow. I pushed them upward and had them grow thick and strong. Once they reached the edge of the window and were a good thickness, I asked the vines to put out branches next to each other, every foot upward and to twine them around together to form a strong vine that we could all step onto and that would also hold our weight.

"A ladder? You grew a ladder? That is so cool," Lark said inspecting it from his place on the ground.

I grinned and said, "Easy."

"Show off," Nora said from her place next to me. She then bumped her hip into my own with just enough force to push me off balance. Then she laughed and got behind Reed, Ash, and Lark, in order to make the climb up to the window.

I let them all struggle up the ladder I'd made, then I grew my own vine. I had it stop right next to my hip to grow thick, then I added in a little fat step I could stand on. I stepped onto the perfect little step and then pushed energy into the plant again and quickly had the vine grow upward until I was standing even with the others.

"No. This is showing off," I said and gave them all a wide smile of pride and humor.

Ash quietly laughed but I could tell he found me funny and enjoyed my quiet show off antics. Nora did as well, but she and Reed had to appear sarcastically stoic. Lark, not sure what to make of me, just stared with a bit of astonishment showing on his face.

"Can we get on with breaking into this place?" Reed asked. He wasn't really waiting for an answer. He was just being…himself.

He tried to lift the window, but it was surprisingly locked.

Ash squeezed in next to him, sharing the same rung on the vine ladder.

I saw how they were on top of each other on that step and asked the vine to widen a bit for them. I added a bit of extra width to grow on the step as well, to make sure it would hold their joined weight.

Then I asked that it not move too fast or sudden as I didn't want them to fall. The vine did as I asked. If anyone wasn't watching, they wouldn't see I was moving it. The vines did push outward, and the step did grow wider and fatter with it.

Both Ash and Reed almost at the same time realized they had more space and could spread out a bit to work on the window. "Thanks, babe," Ash said over his shoulder.

I didn't respond. I just let him do his work.

"It's not anything fancy. It's just a normal window lock. The glass is too. It is not like the stuff they were using on our building to keep us in. We can either try to jimmy it unlocked or just break the glass."

"I say just break it and get it done," Reed said.

"Wait," Nora said. "You guys always want to just go breaking stuff. I think we should try to unlock it first before we go destruction."

"Why do you care if we break something that belongs to them?" Reed asked.

I actually knew where she was going with this, so I stayed quiet and let her explain it.

"I don't," Nora said. "But if we are going to try to get into all four of the buildings we've found, we might not want to tip them off, if possible, especially on the first one, so they don't put up more blocks for us to go through. If we can get in and out of here quietly, the next building should be just as easy."

"Hm," Reed said in answer. Basically, that meant he agreed, in his own form of shorthand. I wanted to laugh but we were still trying to be quiet.

"Okay, the woman makes sense," Lark added. "I was all on board to break everything and anything we wanted too. After what they've done to us all, I think they deserve it and so do we."

"Need any help?" I asked very quietly. I didn't want to take over their plan, but I had an idea if they wanted it.

Reed turned and looked at me with his steady eyes, then said, "Sure. What do you have in mind?"

"Show us what you got," Ash added.

All I did was put my hand on the vine rail of the ladder that was closest to me. What they didn't see was I asked it to put out a tiny little shoot. It was thin and small but was able to slip between the windowpanes right where the lock was. It slid under the weather stripping and was inside. Once inside, I thickened it so it would be strong enough for the task I had in mind.

I had it curl around the handle and pulled the lock downward, easily unlocking the window and allowing us access. Simple, quiet, and a bit showy. I turned my head to smile at the others.

"That was awesome," Lark said.

"Who needs a lock picking set when you have Eve," Ash said. "Are you sure you didn't leave behind a life of crime we don't know about. That was pretty smooth."

I smiled. Didn't agree or deny my previous life. The answer was a boring no. I had not led a life of crime, but they could wonder about it if they wanted to. I wouldn't ruin their fun.

Reed lifted the window all the way open, and one by one we crawled through the opening. When we were standing inside, we gathered close together to discuss our next steps.

"Should we split up in groups," I whispered, "Or stay together?"

Reed looked at each of us one by one, and then said, "I think we should break into two groups. Ash and I can be the lead of each group as we know the technology here. Lark will be a huge help for any group he decides to go with, but we need to get in and out of here as quick as we can. That's why I think groups is a good idea. Anyone disagree?"

I wanted to complain and say we should stay together, but I knew what Reed said was a better plan. As no one put up any argument, we broke into two groups. It was no surprise who each group contained.

I went with Ash, and I guess you could say Lark went with me. Which means Nora went with Reed. Yeah, no shockers on the group split.

My group went to the left and Reed and Nora went to the right.

"Stay on this floor. Meet back here in ten. We will all go through each floor at the same time," Ash said.

We stopped at the first door we came to and swung it open easily. It was an office, and it was being used by someone. However, it looked like a paper pusher type person as it was all just printed copies of emails of no use to us. A sales type.

SaneCorp was big into science, but they made their money by what they created. Mostly, as you imagine, medications and such. There was a real business with a good reputation outside of the shady dealings and experimentation they did under the table in the darkness no one could see.

We intended to bring the dark into the light for all to see.

"Nothing here," Lark said as he quietly closed the file drawer he'd been flipping through.

"Nothing on here either," Ash said, he eyes intent on the computer monitor at the desk as he clicked and moused his way through its contents. "Eve? You find anything?"

I was going through the papers and chaos on the desk and the little credenza against the wall next to it. "No. Nothing here for us," I said.

"Let's head next door," Lark said.

We went room by room and found nothing exciting. When we met back up at the window, Reed asked, "Anything?"

We all shook our heads.

"Us either," Nora said. "Up or down?" She then said. There was one floor above us and a couple below us, so it was a good question.

"Let's go up," Reed said. "That was the big floor in our building."

That was not the big, exciting floor in this building. We went up and found nothing. Then we made our way down to the other floors and still we found nothing. This was just a regular ole SaneCorp administrative building. They did real, above board, business at this location. Bummer.

Nora shrugged and said, "It couldn't be that easy. If we found all we were looking for in the first go, what fun would that be?"

My thoughts? A lot.

"Come on," Reed said, and we all headed back up to the floor we'd come in on. One by one we went out the way we'd come. Locked the window tight, and down we went. Once we all had our feet firmly on the ground, I gave a private thank you to my creation, then I pulled away the life energy I'd given it. I don't know about the others, but I watched as it slowly turned black and began to shrink. Once it turned to ash and blew away in the night, we headed back to the field and crawled our way out.

None of us had anything to say on the drive to our hotel. I figured they were feeling a bit like me and that was let down. We hadn't found a single thing or word of evidence. I was worried we'd destroyed the only building that mattered when we took out Creed and the building we'd been living in.

I didn't mention it to the others, but I was starting to think we, maybe, needed to go back there to see if there was anything left, we could use. I figured I would save that thought, depending on what we found at the other three places. If they were all like this one, we would be done before we knew it with nothing to show for it.

The next day we got up, checked out of the hotel, and were on the road early. We had at least two days of driving to get to the next stop in New Mexico. I sat in the back with Reed and Lark, and I enjoyed some time in my own head.

I was thinking about my past. I started with the little farm I'd had in New Mexico with my friends. They'd known what I was but stayed with me and protected me all the same. I was only a little girl of maybe twelve when I found myself at the sanctuary. They took me in, housed me, and fed me for no reason other than they were good people.

I'd begun helping the harvests, the plants, and animals a little at a time. No one said anything at first, but over time and years they figured it out. They never brought it up, but they understood why I stayed hidden. They never pushed me to go anywhere or meet new people. They helped to keep me hiding as best as they could. Until Reed came looking for me.

He'd talked me into his plan and idea on finding the others. We spent months waiting, but he knew Nora and Ash would come. He was right. They had and our lives changed. Love and friendship were found where we'd been alone and scared for years.

My memories moved on to the mess with Dr. Dane. How in the end he'd been insane with his need for power. We'd killed him out of self-preservation, but it still weighed on my heart. Afterward, there'd been a moment when we thought we were safe. We'd had a time of quiet peace while we lived in the compound with Creed. Until it wasn't anymore. Then we'd destroyed them too.

Maybe we were weapons. Maybe that was our lot in this life. To never find peace. To never be settled with roots. To just be a force of destruction that killed at will.

"Hey," Ash said and nudged me out of my dark thoughts. "Come back to me."

I turned my head and gave him a half smile. It was all I could muster.

"Where were you," he asked.

"Just thinking about the past. My time in New Mexico. Reed and then you and Nora. I was just wondering what the point of us was. If we really were nothing but…death."

"That's not fair," Ash said gently.

"What's fair got to do with it? We are dangerous. We were made to kill and control."

"Yes, but we were made. We did not choose that life. We are fighting to get a better one. We are fighting so we don't have to be that weapon of control and death. We will be more. That's the whole point."

"What if we don't get there? What if we are caught and become exactly that?" I put my hand over my slightly rounded stomach and said, "What about nugget? What if we are caught. What life will they have? Will it be the same one we had growing up?"

"No," Ash said quickly and easily.

"How do you know? How can you have such faith?"

"Because we have each other. We are strong enough to make sure it doesn't happen. I have faith in us. All of us. That's enough."

I took his hand and gave it a squeeze. More as a way of saying I hear you and thank you at the same time. Then I went back to looking out the window. I tried to steer my thoughts away from a dark sad future. I tried to think of what a great place it would be if we could get free. If we could actually put an end to SaneCorp for good.

Chapter Eleven

Two days of driving, two nights of hotels, and many gas station stops later, we arrived in New Mexico.

Our first stop was to find a hotel close to our next destination. There was one a town over that was more worn and older looking than I would have liked, but we wanted to be unknown, and they took cash. Most of the big chains would only rent a room to you if you put a credit card on file.

We didn't want to leave a paper trail, so we needed the old and a little scary, truck stop motel. Sadly. However, because the rooms were really quite small, we rented three rooms. Which means, we all got a little bit of privacy and for Ash and me, a little bit of alone time. I guess Nora and Reed did as well, but I was thinking about me at that moment. I needed a little close time with Ash. Being with all these people day in and day out was starting to wear on me.

I loved my little family but twenty-four seven of family time is too much for anyone. We sat in a car all day, then ate together, and slept together, and there was never any just quiet time. Even in the car when we had nothing to say there was always music going on and the noise of the road. I definitely could use a break.

I flopped down on the double sized bed and just laid there for a moment. Ash came in and dropped his pack. I could sense he was about to start talking so I said, "Shh," and just stayed with my face pressed down against the, hopefully clean, bed spread.

I felt the bed dip with Ash's weight, and he simply curled up behind me and we took a quiet hour to ourselves. He must have needed the break too as he stayed quiet without any real push from me other than the shush.

When it was time to get up and find some dinner, we met up outside our doors, which as we were all right next to each other, was the best place. "How are you holding up," I asked Nora once she exited her room with Reed.

"Not horrible. It's not as dry as I expected but it is hot. I'm going through a lot of water, but all in all not too bad. My stomach feels shaken so I figure maybe I need some bread or something. Calories and carbs are my guess."

"Calories and carbs are the best," I said, and we all walked across the parking lot, then across the street to the little diner that sat there all lit up in the dark of the coming night.

"So, we going out tonight?" Ash asked the group once our food had arrived.

"May as well. We've been cooped up in a car for days. I could use a little exercise and fun," Reed said.

"I'm in," Lark added. "I'm with Reed, I need to do something. So, if we don't go tonight, I may have to run around the block about ten times."

I laughed. Partly because I thought he was joking and partly because maybe he wasn't.

"The sooner we get in and out the sooner I can get out of this hot dry place," Nora said as she downed another class of water. She was not sweating like the rest of us. She used up all her energy trying to keep cool. I loved the warm and hot, but it didn't sap the life out of me the way it did Nora.

"I'm not asking to be mean, but if we get into trouble, will you be able to help?" I asked her.

"No, that's a fair question," she said. "I can help, I just won't have as much to work with. Short burst of power verses anything long and drawn out. Plus, I will wear out fast. I think we should definitely have plenty of water on hand in case we run into issues. I can power back up faster if I have water."

"Then tonight it is," Reed said. "Same game as the last time. Let's hope we get something more usable than we did at the other one. We came away with squat."

I wanted to find something but then again, without knowing what we were really looking for other than evidence of their human experimentation, something could be anything and not always good.

After we ate, we all stopped back at our rooms and got sorted for our next adventure into SaneCorp. I pulled on a pair of leggings this time.

They had a stretchy waistband that would give instead of suffocating me if I had to bend or crawl.

As I was changing, I said to Ash, "I may need to go shopping soon. My clothes are not cutting it in the belly area lately."

He looked up and smiled. "Show me," he asked.

I lifted my shirt to show him what was once a flat tummy, now was a definite muffin top. I was contemplating rolling them down a bit, so they were more on my hips and not my waist, but I was worried they wouldn't stay up then.

Ash stood up and cupped his hand over my rounding belly. "This is really cute," he said. "There is just something about seeing you like this that makes me happy."

After a moment he asked, "How's our nugget doing?"

"As far as I know, fine. I am trying not to connect to them very much. You know I want our baby to have as normal a growth cycle as possible. If I pass along any energy, I can speed it up. It is possible to do that, and I don't want to for them."

"Can you feel it yet?" he asked.

I shook my head. "Not yet. I figure not long now though. I'm about four months. I figure any time now, I should get the butterfly feeling in there. Or that's what the books I'm reading say."

"How long until I can feel it?"

"Maybe you should be getting books too," I said teasing him just a little bit.

He understood my humor and didn't take offense. "Maybe I should," he said looking into my eyes. I waited as he slowly lowered his head and waited even more with bated breath for his lips to descend over mine.

One of the first things I always think of when Ash kisses me is there is a spark of our energy connecting that I feel from the top of my head all the way down through my toes. I feel like I am being lit from within each and every time.

I sank into him. He wrapped his arms around me and held me close. His warmth cocooning me, allowing me to feel safe and loved. "Ash," I whispered.

"Hm," he said as he pressed his face against my bare neck.

"I love you," I said.

"I love you too," he said.

I giggled as his voice rumbled against my neck and tickled. "No, I mean, yes, I love you, but I mean it's more than just because we are supposed to. I love you for who you are, for how you make me feel, for the future I see, and so many things. I just wanted you to know that.

"I know what you are saying. We were created for each other, but I don't love you because of that. I love you because you are so giving and nurturing, which I need. I love how you see the world and how you want to make it better. I love how you take the hard moments in stride and find the good in everything. I love you, Eve. Not some connection made by SaneCorp."

I gave him a quick hug and then said, "I guess we better get a move on."

"Yep. Next stop…SaneCorp."

I pulled on a pair of sneakers, and we headed out.

Like the last time, we drove out to the SaneCorp Building and parked not quite a mile away. This building, like all the others was the same basic style and structure. It was again lit up in the night. The lights could be seen from where we stood almost a mile away. However, this building was not in a fallow field.

This one was in a pine tree forest. It was thick with old trees. We could tell the trees were old as they all had broken branches at least ten feet up and then new branches of pine needles filled out until the top. The trees were also in pretty straight lines so maybe it had been a tree farm in the past. Maybe not, but the saying of, God doesn't create in straight lines, always stuck with me.

Regardless of where the forest came from, it did provide us with some cover. We enjoyed a nice walk in the middle of the night through the quiet forest. I reached out to see and hear what creatures were around us.

My hand was in Ash's as we walked so, I closed my eyes and reached out with my senses. There was a small herd of deer behind us. A lone fox creeping about in the night. Birds sleeping quietly in nests, and even a bull elk not far to our right. I spent some time checking him out as he could be dangerous. He didn't seem to even care about our being in his territory. I didn't sense any bears or mountain lions thankfully. Maybe they were smart enough to stay away from areas of people.

"What do you see," Ash whispered in my ear.

"Birds," I said. "I wish I knew what they were. All I can sense is what they are. I can't see them. There is an elk over there," I said pointing.

"Is that bad," he asked.

"Is what bad?" Lark asked.

"There's an elk over there," I said answering Lark. Then for Ash, I said, "No, it's not bad. He's enjoying the quiet of the forest and doesn't really care about us at all. We aren't bothering him so he's not bothering us. He seems peaceful."

"Anything we should be worried about," Reed asked. He'd stopped and waited for us to catch up with him and Nora who had been leading our little pack.

"No. Not that I can sense. Everyone is quiet except for the fox. He's hungry," I said.

"Good to know," Nora said. She was huffing a bit. Even in the night it was still pretty warm. The humidity was low which for me and the others was great, but it made Nora more uncomfortable.

"You doing okay?" I asked.

She took a deep breath and said, "Yeah, I just wish we parked a little closer. I'm tired and hot and I hate it."

Without any planning we all stopped just inside the forest where it ended. I had my hands on my hips, and I would admit to myself I was a little out of breath too. I was feeling out of shape as it was harder to breathe with exertion than it used to be. What was that all about?

"You know how fast-food restaurants all look the same. Apparently, SaneCorp took a page out of their book as all these buildings look exactly the same. Five stories high. Windows spaced evenly across each floor. Plain white stone on the outside. They have no imagination."

Nora laughed and said, "At least we know the layout. We can get in and get out."

We stood there for a moment more. I used those seconds to just feel out the building. Every time we came to one of these, I would have a moment of dread and fear hit, then I could push it aside and move forward.

"You all ready?" Nora asked. "Cause, I need out of this stinking heat!"

"Yeah," I said. I was as ready as I was going to get.

"Let's go then," Lark said and took the lead. My brother fit in nicely with my little family. They took him in and accepted him for what he was…he was one of us even if he was not as damaged as we were. Oh, I know many would say we were gifted not damaged, but some days, my sad dark days, I knew it wasn't true.

I hurried to catch up to him. His long strides took up a lot of ground next to my smaller ones. I touched his arm, and he slowed and turned to me. I smiled and said, "I just wanted to tell you, I love you. I'm so glad you found me."

He grabbed my hand and gave it a quick squeeze before letting it go. He then said with a big toothy showing grin "I know it. Now get those little legs a-moving. We got bad guys to take down."

"Bad guys…Lark this is not cops and robbers," I replied with a quiet chuckle.

"Maybe that is exactly what it is little sis." He quickened his pace again and all I could do was feel the warm joy at his presence.

It's funny but I had missed him. Even though I did not remember anything about him, I felt fuller and complete now that he was with me again. My mind may not have known about him, but my heart did. It felt the missing even when I didn't know it.

We headed toward the back again and stood facing the building looking up at the windows. "Same drill?" Reed asked.

I shrugged and said, "Why bother? There are windows right here. We can break in just as easy from the ground and we know where the cameras are now."

"We think we do," Ash said.

"Hmm, she's kinda right. There is no reason to waste the energy creating a ladder when we can just get in from the ground level," Reed said.

"Okay, come on then," Ash agreed easily.

I smiled as I stepped up to the window and, using my vines, I unlocked it easily and in we went.

Lark and Reed went in first. Then Nora climbed in behind them. As soon as she was inside, she let out a long and breathy sigh and said, "Ah, much better." Apparently, the AC was working just fine.

I smiled as I stepped over the sill and into the building and a smell hit me. I backed up and whispered, "Wait!"

Every single one of the others froze. They didn't ask questions. They didn't argue. They simply stopped moving instantly and took what I said seriously. I lifted my head up a bit and took a deep breath of the air inside that building. I put out feelers of my energy to try to pick up anything out of the ordinary.

Ash came to my side and waited quietly.

I pushed a little harder with my gift and when the realization hit, everyone saw it on my face. I turned to Ash with wide, and maybe a bit scared, eyes.

"What is it?" He asked me. He said those three words so calmly. I think, had he been panicked like I was feeling I might have really freaked out, but instead he was easy and trusting of me to figure it out.

"It's a dim, almost not there, life," I said so quietly only Ash could hear me. I wasn't trying to hide it from the others. I was trying to hide it from myself. If I said it loud, it would be real. I didn't want it to be real.

"What do you mean?" He asked.

"What?" Reed asked. "Eve, what is it?"

I shook my head at them and said, "I'm not certain but…I think there is someone down there." I pointed to the door we all knew was to the staircase that led to the basement level. "I think they are dying or maybe they are trying to live. I don't know other than it's very faint."

"What should we do?" Lark asked the question.

I took a moment to connect eyes with each of them, before I said, "I think we have a decision to make. We can either let them die, or we can help them live."

"What do you think we should do," Reed asked me.

"I think we should leave it alone," Nora said. "We don't even know who or what it is. I don't want any of us in danger."

"We are always in danger," I said. "That's our life. I think we should go see what it is and then, we can decide. They might be exactly what we are looking for."

"Eve, honey. We all know if it's a dying animal, you will want to save it. So, if we go down there, we are going to help. The question is, do we go down?"

"Ash, I can't change who I am. You guys have to decide this one. I'll go with whatever the group decides, but I can't make this choice for all of us."

"I know who you are, babe. I know exactly," Ash said. He turned to the others and asked, "What do you all think?"

Lark stood with his hands on his hips and looked from one to another of us. "How is there even a decision to make. Whatever it is needs help. We have to go down."

Lark was so much like me. He had such a helping caring soul. "I don't know if I can save it," I said.

"You can heal, we all saw you do it," Reed said.

"I can heal burns and hurts from the outside; I have no idea what this creature is facing other than death. I don't know that I can heal death."

"Only one way to find out" Nora said with a shrug. "Let's get this over with." Then as the decision was finally made, she turned and went to the doorway, and we all followed behind her down the stairs into the basement hallway. It was dark down there.

The smell that set me off when we first entered the building had been very faint. It was much stronger in that hallway. I hadn't been nauseous in a few days, but the smell was definitely setting me off. "Ugh, the smell," I said and covered my nose.

"I don't smell anything," Reed said. He sniffed strong through his nose. "Yeah, nothing."

"Me either," Nora said.

Ash took hold of my hand in that darkness and said, "What does it smell like?"

My brain was searching through memories and knowledge to put the smell in place. "I'm not sure," I said but then, the answer snapped into place. "It smells of dead."

I saw the dark outline of Reed step in close to Nora and they linked hands too. "Stay close together guys. We may have the evidence right here we're looking for."

I knew we were wanting to find evidence of the illegal acts being done by SaneCorp, but I was very afraid right then of what that evidence might be. I was praying to myself it was not a giant pile of dead bodies. I didn't think I could take it.

"Should we find the lights," Lark asked. It was part a real question and part sarcasm as why were we standing around in the dark, in a basement, with no windows?

"Ash? Can you detect any cameras? I don't," Reed said.

"I don't see any sign of them, or any lights up in the corners. Eve, can you feel any cameras?"

"I don't know. All I can feel is the fluttering life down here. It's overtaking everything else."

"Let's chance it then," Nora said. We all felt around the walls to find a switch. Someone must have found it as the hallway was suddenly illuminated. We all squinted at one another while our eyes adjusted.

Once we were ready, Lark said, "Eve, lead the way."

I didn't want to, but as I was the only one who could sense where to go, it was up to me. "Lark, can you feel it?"

"No," he said simply.

I took hold of his hand like I used to do when we were kids and shared my energy with him so he could feel it too.

He stopped in his tracks and pressed a hand against his heart.

"What?" Ash asked.

"I can feel it," Lark said. "We should hurry though. It's suffering."

I patted his shoulder and tugged him forward.

At the very end of the hallway there was a set of two metal doors. "This is new," Ash said.

"Not your standard SaneCorp design," Reed added.

I tried the door. "It's locked," I said.

"Scoot over," Ash said as he shouldered his way in front of me and Lark to get a look at the door lock. "Yeah, I can get this one."

We stood there outside the door as Ash made quick work of unlocking it. Then we swung open the big doors as quietly as possible and stepped inside.

"Oh," Nora said and put a hand over her nose and mouth. "I can smell it now." Her words were a bit mumbled under her hand, but we all knew what she said. The anxious energy in the room was starting to overwhelm me. I think I was projecting too much on Lark to, as I felt his heart speed up.

I quickly let go of his hand and removed my projection from his. He turned and gave me a knowing smile and shrugged a bit. "Sorry. I'm not used to all this anymore. It's hard to absorb."

"Don't be sorry. It's hard for me too and I do it all the time."

The room itself was still dark but for the light falling in from the hallway. I crept forward on silent feet, more by the sense of the life energy pulling at me than by sight. Against the far wall, there were metal crates with bars like you would find in a lab with animals.

"Is it a monkey?" Reed asked.

I would have agreed with him as that was what it appeared to be, but he didn't have the extra senses I did when it came to energy. "It doesn't feel like a monkey," I replied and continued forward.

"Oh, God," Nora said from behind me. I heard footsteps hurry over to the side and retch.

The smell had increased from death and added in urine and other things I didn't want to accept, including the metallic sent of blood. I pulled my phone out of my back pocket and turned on the little flashlight.

"I'm sorry, I can't," Nora said weakly.

A cool and very gentle breeze caressed my face. I hesitated. Where did it come from?

It grew in strength. My hair blew back away from my face as churning air moved through the room all around us in a circle. It gathered the stale repugnant air and dragged it out the wide-open steal doors behind us. Then the force of the wind calmed. However, there continued to be an easy breeze through the room.

It had taken only seconds, but the wind had cleared the room of the stench of death and everything else. "Reed?" I asked and turned to look at him. My little light giving off just enough illumination I could see him if not his features. He was standing over to the side with Nora wrapped protectively in his arm. He didn't say a word. He only slowly shook his head back and forth.

I looked to Ash and Lark and both of them also shook their heads. We all had a feeling though. We didn't know where the wind came from, but we knew who we were and what we were doing here.

"Please," I whispered oh so very softly. I don't know what I was praying for or even to. Maybe it was just a way of wishing out loud that what I was about to see wouldn't destroy me.

I crept forward again toward the crates on the back wall. Ash and Lark were right behind me. In fact, Ash was almost on top of me. I whipped my head around and glared at him. He smiled and didn't move off even an inch.

My light moved along the floor and then up to the crate that I felt the energy from. There was a large dark shadow huddled inside. It was large for an animal, but small for a person. I moved forward a bit further then gasped as I saw a bare leg. A bare, human leg, bruised, cut, and covered in dirt and filth from who knows what, but the leg was definitely human.

I moved the light upward to find a pale face with dark eyes, wide as saucers, staring directly at me. "Ash," I said, my voice shaking on that one word.

I rushed forward along with Lark and Ash, but Lark shoved me aside and raced to the cage. Lark had pushed me so hard that I tumbled over and fell to the ground. That all by itself was strange, but then as he grabbed the bars on the cage and tried to yank them open, I grew concerned.

Lark turned to face me and now Ash who'd come over to check on me. "What the hell, man!" Ash snarled.

"Ash! You gotta help her. Get her out!" Lark begged.

It was the tone and the begging voice that scared me. "Wait," I said and grabbed Ash's shirt to hold him back. "Something wrong here."

Ash looked around the room. "I don't see anything. What do you feel?"

Reed and Nora were now up with me, and Ash and we all watched in almost horror as Lark yanked and pulled on the door almost mindlessly. "We gotta get her out of there. Eve she's hurt and in pain."

"Lark," I said standing up. I went over to him and slowly and very gently placed my hand on his arm and pushed real energy into him. I needed to know what was going on to make him so erratic and frantic. I jerked my hand off him and back up quickly.

"It's a trap," I said and ran to Ash. "We need to go."

"Whoa, hey, how do you know?"

"Look at Lark," I said. "He's desperate to get to her. A person he has never laid eyes on before, who is covered in filth, and who seems to be close to death. He's desperate."

"So?" Reed said.

"Really look at him," I said. All of them did as I'd told them to do. The broken girl had her eyes focused, intent on Lark, and Lark only, and he was just as focused on her. You couldn't see much of her other than she was naked and had big sad eyes. Her hair was long and dark but that could be because of how gross and filthy she was. For all we knew her hair was as white as snow. It covered part of her face and hung down in clumps to the floor of the crate. Lark had his hands fisted on the bars. His face was now pressed into them. "Please, Ash. Help me," he said.

"They're bonded," Nora said softly.

I nodded. "They know. They know Lark has some of my gifts. They know about him. They created a pair for him. They knew we would come, and they knew he was with us. He would find her. This is a trap. We have to get out."

SaneCorp in all their screwed-up wisdom, gave us a gift when they made us. There were four of us, two boys and two girls. While changing our make-up and our DNA, they created a pairing between one boy and one girl. Each would be drawn to that one person. Attracted to them in a way we would never be with anyone else. We would need them as they would need us. These pairs were me with Ash and Nora with Reed.

It was all still somewhat new for us, and we were still trying to figure it out. What we did know is that it was a gift in some ways and a curse in others. We had a person that would, as the saying goes, walk through fire for us, but it was also a detriment in that, that one person could be used against us. If someone threatened our person, we would do and give up almost anything and everything for them. So, we were strong as pairs, but also weak in some ways too.

The other detriment is that in this pairing we would likely one day have children. I would guess that SaneCorp hoped that these children would be naturally gifted. The parents would pass on their mutated DNA and create another generation of superhuman beings. The new generation could possibly get a mixing of the two gifts of their parents, or maybe a new power all of their own. The idea that we were all part of this plan of procreation scared me in many ways. I was falling right into their hands and could possibly be giving them the future weapon they were all desperately hoping for, in the form of my precious child.

"We can't leave her." Ash said. "I have a feeling if we tried, Lark won't come with us."

Ash suddenly grabbed his head and turned to me with frightened eyes. "What!" I pretty much shouted.

"You know how I told you when Creed was trying to get into my head there was sort of a tickle that I sensed?"

"Yeah."

"I am feeling that now."

"I don't feel anything. Nora?" I asked.

She shook her head, but Reed stepped forward and said, "Me too."

"Walls up, everyone," Ash said, and we all knew what he meant. It was how we had stopped Creed from reading our minds. We thought of something blocking, such as a wall or a dark room. It was a way to only allow that thought into our minds and someone trying to get in, would not be able to. All they would see is what we pictured. Or that was what we thought would happen. It had seemed to work with Creed. It was also all we had to go on, so we just did what we knew.

I used a wall covered in ivy as my blocker. It was not always easy to hold that thought. It was like trying to multi-task without a brain.

I ran to Lark and tried to get him to hear me and said, "We need to go."

He looked into my eyes, and said, "I'm not going anywhere without her. Get her out, and we can leave. Otherwise, I'm staying."

I looked around desperately knowing this was bad and knowing we had to leave, but I was not going without my brother. I was not leaving him. "Ash?"

"On it," he said and stepped up to the lock on the crate door and went to work.

I stood right behind him and Lark. Both of us were watching the girl inside. I didn't sense evil so to speak, but I did sense rage. I didn't even blame her for the red-hot emotion either, but I was not certain she wouldn't lash out at us with it. After all, she didn't know us.

Her eyes were focused on Lark and his on hers. I felt a pulsing of light energy in the air between them. At first, I thought it was just their life sparks, but then I focused on it further and found it had a back-and-forth movement of it. It would stay with one for a moment or two and then pass to the other where it also stayed a moment or so, before it went back.

My eyes widened as I realized what was happening. I grabbed Lark's arm and demanded his attention. "Can you communicate with her?"

"Yes," he said shortly. Just that one word and nothing else, but when I say chills ran down by spine, I mean they zipped down it like cold lightning.

"What is she saying?" I asked half afraid he wouldn't tell me.

"She is saying, please don't leave her," he said simply.

"Got it," Ash said as I heard the locked click open. Lark shoved to the front, and before we could caution him, he swung it open and reached inside.

I held my breath, ready to attack and ready to protect us all, but the girl didn't move. Not a muscle. She hardly breathed as he gently slipped his hands and arms under her to lift her out. "Eve, hurry. Help her." It was a demand and yet it was a desperate request. I couldn't say no.

He turned with her in his arms, and we all got our first real look at her. She was small. More than just thin, but small in size overall. Her hair was long, and so tangled and knotted, I really couldn't tell how long. I would guess it was like mine and sat comfortably around her waistline. I also wasn't certain of the color as it was filthy. I would guess a light brown, but

I'd have to wait and see after she was clean. Her eyes were big and blue. They seemed ginormous in contrast to her small features. It was hard to see her expression in the small light we had, but she was very pretty to look at. Even dirty, abused, and hurt, I could tell she was lovely. She also was almost naked as she had only scraps of clothing on her. Tattered and torn and minuscule. I wasn't sure the pieces of fabric would even stay on her body if she stood.

He placed her down on an empty metal table, which reminded me of an autopsy table you see on tv. I don't know if that is what it was, but I didn't know if it wasn't either. All I really knew for certain was it was probably cold.

The slight breeze that had stayed steadily blowing the entire time picked up force the moment Lark released her. "She's scared," he said simply.

"She's scared?" I whispered for Ash to hear alone.

Ash took my hand and gave it a squeeze. "I'm right here with you, babe."

"Can you fix her?" Lark asked.

I didn't respond right away as I needed to have a look at her. I pushed a small burst of energy and studied her inside and out. "She's mostly hungry and thirsty to the point of severe dehydration and starvation. Nora, can you get her some water?"

"Yep," she said and set to the task.

"What is she saying Lark? Will she let me touch her?" I asked because she was cringing from me. She was like a cornered lion about to strike. Weak and broken or not, her eyes and fierce expression told me that she could do harm if she needed to.

"I'm telling her you can help her, but she's really scared," Lark said.

"Can she speak at all?" I asked.

After a moment when I assumed he was asking her my question, he said, "I'm not sure. I think she knows how, she just hasn't in so long it's easier for her to use her mind."

"Is that her gift? Telepathy? She can communicate with people through their minds?" Reed asked.

"And the wind?" Nora added. "She can obviously bring that to the table. It was a welcome gift there when we first came in. I'm not going to mince words, as it was rank in here."

"Nora," I said.

"It was. She can read minds, so she would know it."

"She says she can't read your and Eve's minds. Just Reed's, Ash's, and mine," Lark said.

I laid a gentle hand on her leg closest to me. I needed to feel where the damage was in order to push my healing waves toward it. She flinched, but she didn't pull away.

"Even with our wall block?" Ash asked sounding a little miffed.

"Yeah," Lark said.

Ash turned to face her directly and said, "That's rude. Don't do that to me again."

"Hey," Lark said.

"I don't care why. I don't care who. You don't go poking around in people's heads without their permission. I took out Creed for doing that. I mean it, Lark. Get it through to her I don't play that game. I doubt Reed will either."

No tears fell from her eyes, most likely as she was too dehydrated to form them, but I bet if she could they would have been flowing.

Nora stepped up and placed a glass beaker filled with water to the girl's lips. She drank and drank until it was empty. "Let that settle first and then I will get you more. I don't want you to get sick from drinking too much too fast."

"Eve?" Lark asked again.

"Working on it, little brother. Patience," I said. I was working my way from her toes to the legs I was touching, upward to her torso. I healed the bruised and broken places as I went. There wasn't a lot of life ending damage to her, but there was a lot of painful torture type damage. Several toes on her feet were broken. Her muscles and tendons around her knees showed damage as if they'd been dislocated at one point. Her kidneys were bruised. Her intestines were empty. Shriveled up empty as if she'd not had food for a long time. I healed all the places I could. Her heart was strong. Her mind was busy.

As I progressed through her body, I felt her getting stronger. I couldn't feel her thoughts or see into her mind like she could the boys. I could feel her emotions though. She was vacillating between fear, anger, thankfulness and one that was a bit confusing to me, regret. As I healed her and the pain receded, she became less rigid in her position and how she held her body.

She softened. Her breathing became stronger and less labored. I realized as she began to breathe more normally, it had hurt to breathe so she'd been holding it back and slowing it down to ease her pain. How long had she been like this.

She couldn't cry but apparently, I could cry enough for the both of us. Her poor abused body was breaking my heart. "Does she have a name?" I asked quietly.

"Star," Lark said.

"I got you, Star," I said. "I know there is more to do, but now that you are stronger, I think we need to get out of here. Lark, lift her up and let's get a move on."

"Wait, we haven't gone through the place. We need evidence, Eve," Reed said.

I looked at Lark and then to Star and said, "Fine. Lark, you take Star and head toward the car. You are going to have to carry her. She's too weak to walk, let alone run. Take it slow and just get her there safely. We will do a quick run through of the place and get what we can."

"Let's go. I think we should split up again this time. You and Ash and me and Nora. Get a move on Lark. Call if you run into trouble," Reed said.

I placed my hand on Star's shoulder and felt her calming emotions. She felt almost hopeful. I could tell by the energy waving between them that she and Lark were still talking to one another. "Be safe," I told Lark. Star may have seemed calm, but we didn't know her. I didn't know her. I still believed with my entire being that this was a trap, and we were either staying in it waiting for it to spring shut or we were bringing the trap with us in the form of an injured girl.

"We will," Lark replied and held her tight against him.

I watched them with very real trepidation as they walked out of the room. "Let's get this done," I said and hurriedly moved toward the door as well.

I got more and more nervous as we went through that building. We found nothing. I mean every room looked used, but there was nothing on the computers. At all. They ran and they had applications and programs on them but there was not one saved file on any of them we looked at.

There were not any files or papers at all in the offices. Blank paper galore and lots of extra supplies in the supply rooms, but nothing to show for it. It was like the place was wiped clean except for the one single piece of big giant evidence we found that we couldn't even use. That evidence was Star and we'd taken her with us. Ash got her out of her prison. I'd healed her. Lark carried her right out.

I'd say it was a wasted trip except for Star, but she made me nervous. As the four of us climbed out of the building and made our way to the car I asked the burning question of, "So? What do you think of Star?"

"It's convenient, I'll say that for certain," Reed said.

"And too easy," Ash added.

"Is she a pawn, or a spy, or maybe an assassin? Nora said.

"Exactly," I said.

The rest of the walk back to the car was silent. Lark and Star were sitting on the ground next to the car when we arrived. Star was cuddled close to Lark on his lap. She appeared even smaller in that moment than she had in the cage. Lark's arms were relaxed around her tiny body.

As it was dark out, we still could not get a good look at her. The moon light was shrouded by the forest, so although it was not quite as dark as it had been in that room, it was still dark enough to not get a real solid look.

"We have a slight problem," Lark said.

"What now?" Ash asked? I felt immediate anxiety at Lark's easily spoken works.

"How are we all going to fit in the car? It was a tight fit with five. Now we have six," he said.

"Oh," I said and looked at the car. I had not thought of that.

"She will have to sit on your lap till I can boost us a bigger car," Nora said.

"No," I said. "No, stealing."

"Eve, we don't have time to hunt down a new bigger car. We need to just get out of town here and get home and sort out what's going on and what our next move is," Nora said.

"She's right, honey," Ash said.

I looked to Reed to see his thoughts on the matter. He looked at the car and then at us then said, "Okay, I'll drive. Lark and Star can sit up front with her on his lap. The rest in the back. We will get back to our hotel, and I will get up early and find us a new car."

"Works for me," I said happily.

"Reed, we don't have…" Nora started to say but Reed cut her off.

"We have a long drive to get home. I don't want to be driving a stolen car with a person that we don't even know if she exists on paper. I'm not explaining to some cop how we have a bruised and broken girl in our car who has no ID or anything. We are lucky she has some clothes on." He turned to Lark and asked, "She does have clothes on, right?"

"Barely," Lark replied.

"Well, that's one thing," I said.

"Okay, let's get out of here and to the hotel. It's lucky we got extra rooms," Nora said. "You think she's okay staying with Lark tonight?"

I turned to Lark and said, "Good question. Lark?"

He focused on Star and after a moment of their mental discussion he said, "Yes. She's staying with me tonight."

I looked her in the eye and asked, "Are you good with that?" I wanted her to say that was what she wanted. I trusted my brother, but I didn't trust her at.

Star nodded her head once in agreement. I left it at that. We piled in the car, with Reed in the driver's seat, Lark in the passenger seat with Star on his lap, and the rest of us stuffed in the backseat. Thankfully we only had a short way to go like that. All we needed was to get pulled over with an over filled car, and as Reed put it, a broken girl, without any ID, who didn't talk.

She could talk though. Lark had said she could. She was going to have to get used to doing that again. I was not and I don't think the others were going to be thrilled with having to go through Lark every time one of us wanted to talk to her.

Chapter Twelve

We arrived at the hotel, and we all went into our separate rooms. Once inside ours, I turned to Ash and asked, "What do you think of her?"

He shrugged. "I'm holding my judgement for the time being."

"Why? What is giving you concern?" I asked. I wanted to know if it was the same thing as me, but I didn't want to bias his concerns with my own by telling him what I thought.

"She tried to read our minds. I hate that she did that. It's intrusive and creepy and honestly, I find it evil. You don't get to just poke around inside someone's brain without a thought to asking if it is okay. Creed did that to us. I won't allow it again," he said.

"I knew that was an issue for you. I didn't like it either, but I want to give her the benefit of the doubt and think maybe she doesn't know any better."

"Maybe," he said as he toed off his shoes, and removed all his clothes but for his boxers. "I still don't like it. Plus, you mentioned it was awful convenient she was there and nothing else was. Then it's funny we were the ones to find her, and we are the ones to get her out. It feels like she could be a plant."

I'd told them all that. I'd felt it from the first flash of energy it was a trap.

Ash got into bed and motioned for me to join him. I slipped out of my shoes and leggings and crawled in next to him and positioned myself up against his side with my leg tossed over his body. He was nice and warm against my air chilled skin. He smelled like pines.

"You smell like the forest," I said softly in the darkness of the room. "Were you climbing those trees in the forest?" I said as a joke, simply because I liked the idea of him climbing trees. Up high in the branches, free to do as he pleased. Free to climb, or sit, or just enjoy the air.

He must have liked the idea too as he chuckled. It sounded loud in my ear against his body. "No, but I did lean against the ones at the edge of the clearing while we checked the place out. Maybe I have sap on me? Should have showered, but I'm exhausted. It's been a long day."

"No, I like it," I said. Then after a moment I added, "We just need to be careful around her."

"We also need to make sure she is not carrying a tracking device," Ash said.

I sat up and said, "No! You really think she's that dirty?"

"Not sure if she is or not yet. But she could be carrying one on her or even in her and she wouldn't know it," he said.

I sat silent, mulling it all over in my head. "Someone needs to tell Lark, as I have a feeling, we aren't getting close to her without his consent."

"Did you feel any sort of tracker on her when you were healing her?"

"No, but I wasn't looking for that type of energy. I was looking for emotion type of energy not technology type."

"Is there a difference? Isn't energy, energy?" He asked.

"No. One, the emotion one, feels…thick and condensed. The technology type is airy and light," I said. "It's hard to explain, I guess."

"You should try to feel her out tomorrow," Ash said.

"Yeah," I agreed. "I'll see what I can do."

I closed my eyes and let sleep finally claim me. It had been a long day and now a long night. How early was Reed going to get up to go car hunting? No idea. I hope he didn't need me to do anything. I wanted to sleep for a week, that is how tired I was.

Bone and brain weary.

The next morning came not as early as I feared, but earlier than I wanted. We'd finally gotten to sleep around two thirty in the morning and it was only nine a.m. "Dude," I said when Ash shook me awake, "it can't be time to get up."

He laughed loud and happily and said, "And yet, it is. Come on sleepy head, we have miles to cover to get us home."

"Ugh," was my only response.

I did get up though. I pulled on a pair of light shorts and realized I could not comfortably button them. I sighed.

"What?" Ash asked.

"My shorts don't fit," I replied with a look of forlorn sadness directed at him for good measure.

"Let me see," he said and came to kneel in front of me and look at the button and the expanse between it and its buttonhole. "Yeah, that's a problem. Can you just leave them undone?"

"No, they won't stay up if I do that."

He stared at the button for a second then asked, "You have a hair thing?"

"Yes," I said and stepped over to my pack and grabbed a small elastic hair band and handed it over to him.

He secured the hair tie first to the button, then slipped the tail into the buttonhole, and then looped it over the button. I looked at it and saw it created a nice little expandable tie for my pants. They'd stay up and didn't suffocate me at the same time. I laughed out loud and said, "You are a genius sometimes."

He smiled up at me from where he kneeled before me and said, "All the time."

~ * ~

"This is a piece of junk," Lark said looking disgusted at the multi-colored and hard rusted Honda parked before us.

"How old is this?" Ash asked as he circled around the vehicle.

He was holding back a smile. I could see it in the clenched muscles of his jaw. He found entertainment in the strangest of things. It was in these moments I wished I could communicate through my mind to Ash. Not the rest of the world, but to Ash, most definitely. I wanted to know what was so funny.

"Look, I know it looks like a piece of shit, but it has a good engine. It will get us home," Reed said. There was obvious annoyance in his voice. Maybe that was why it was funny to Ash. He did enjoy frustrating Reed.

"Then you drive it," Lark said.

"Dude, did you come out with me at the butt crack of dawn to hunt up a car? No. I was the one that went out and did the job. Maybe you could just say thanks!" Reed was definitely not a happy camper. However, he was kinda right though.

"Thank you, Reed. I really do appreciate you," I said. It was first and foremost very true. However, I also wanted to try to defuse the situation if possible. The air was heavy with unhappy emotions. It was making me antsy.

"I would have come, if you'd asked," Lark added.

Reed took a menacing step toward him and said, "I did! I knocked on your door first thing this morning with no response! You want to make choices in our group, then maybe start thinking of the group and not yourself."

"Whoa," Nora said. "Let's dial it down a bit."

I jumped in too and said, "We are all tired and cranky. I say we get on the road and find some breakfast."

Reed and Lark stared at one another for a long tense moment, before Lark finally broke the contest and said, "Fine."

He then went and got Star from the room. As they stepped outside, Star was still a bit wobbly on her feet. As she came into the light, we all finally got a real look at her. All I could think was whoo, she was a looker. Her hair now clean and brushed, came down not quite to her waist. It was shiny and thick and mostly brown. What made it gorgeous was it was mixed with golden highlights. Not from a bottle either. Those were all natural to her.

Her eyes appeared just as big and just as blue as the night before, but they seemed to hold less darkness and fear. I noticed she was about my height, but her frame was very small. She fit very nicely with Lark and his larger, lighter looks.

Lark had very light brown hair. It was more like a dirty blond type of brown. Not really either color, but lighter than the dark of Star's.

As I watched them both, I realized neither of them had the pale skin that I, and Ash, Reed, and Nora had. We had pale, pale skin. We had decided it was a side effect of the experimentation we'd been though. We got awesome powers and gifts, but we were lacking in other ways, this being one of them. It's hard to explain how light we were, but I'd noticed we sometimes looked almost a very light almost-not-there pink or purple at times. Although we didn't tan, we didn't burn either, so there was that. But we certainly were missing color. Lark and Star though, they had a warm complexion. I think it would be called peaches and creme. Regardless, I decided that was not fair.

Lark went around to the passenger side and helped Star into the new to us but very old car. Reed and Nora stepped over to the other car. I turned to Ash and silently asked, what he wanted to do. See this would have been a good time for that mind talking thing. If we picked Reed and Nora to ride with, it would alienate Lark and Star. If we picked Lark and Star, it would be like we were choosing and backing them over Reed. I didn't want to split up, but I didn't know what to do either.

I pleaded with Nora with my eyes, asking her for help. She must have felt the mood of the group too as she turned to Reed and said, "Why don't you and Ash take the lead. Me and Eve can pack in with the others and get to know Star a little better."

Nora liked to be seen as tough and hard as nails, but she was just an ole softy on the inside. "That is a great idea," I chimed in and headed over to Lark before Ash could argue.

"Scooch up Lark, so I can get in." I said as I slid between the driver's seat and into the back seat. The Honda was not only a hunk of junk it only had two doors, so getting in the back was a hassle. "Come on, Nora."

"There is a pancake type place about ten miles up. Stop there," Nora said to Reed. She gave him a quick kiss and I think whispered something in his ear before she turned to me and climbed in the back next to me. "Let's go," she said happily.

I felt the fake of it though. That's one of the benefits and problems with my new and improved gifts. I could really tell when people were lying. Even if it was for the benefit of the group, I felt it. I wondered if Lark was as strong in that area. Did he feel it too?

I made eye contact with him in the rear-view mirror and realized, yes. He did.

Thankfully we made our way to the little diner in quiet ease. Breakfast was a bit on the silent side, but it was not awful. We were back in the cars and on our way home within an hour. "So, tell us about yourself," I said to Star after we'd been in the car for about half an hour.

I wanted to know who she was. How did she get mixed up with SaneCorp. How did she end up in that cage? Did she know about us? All the nuts and bolts of how she ended up in that basement room for us to conveniently find.

"She said it's a long story," Lark answered for her.

Nora frowned. "You said she could talk, right?"

"She says it easier for her to just mind speak to me," he said.

"Well…it's not easier for us," I said gently. "It's hard to have a conversation with you as an intermediary."

"Maybe when she's stronger," he said.

I glanced at Nora and frowned. She did the same to me. It was going to be a long drive.

We drove straight on for about two'ish hours before I needed a break. The silence in the car was too loud. I would not believe it if any of the others in the car said they didn't feel the same way. You didn't need to be special to feel the heavy weight of the silence in that car. "Let's pull off and get out for a bit," I said and texted Ash to say the same.

He responded right away. "Ash said there is a mall up ahead a few miles. Take exit twenty-three and follow them. They will lead the way," I said.

We found the food court in the mall, and all grabbed something to eat. I stayed with a rice bowl and the others seemed to go for sandwiches.

"How's the drive going?" Ash asked us all.

"Silent," Nora said.

I wanted to object, but I was a little frustrated with that too.

"Why? There are four of you in the car? Three, girls. How in the world was it silent?" Reed asked.

I scrunched my face at him and said, "Just was. I think I will catch the next leg of the journey with you if you don't mind."

"Sorry Lark, I'm out too," Nora said. "I can't take much more of that."

Ash and Reed looked from Nora and I, to Lark and Star. "Okay, what is going on?" Ash asked.

I sighed loud and heavy and said, "It's like playing a game of telephone without the fun and laughter."

"She can talk," Lark said defiantly. "She just doesn't want to right now."

"Well, that is just peachy for her. It's tedious and rude for the rest of us," I said with my own annoyance showing.

"Hey," Ash said and looked around uneasily. "Let's not do this here."

"Why not?" I snarled.

"Cause…flowers," Reed said and indicated my feet where one little white daisy was popping through the grout of the tile flooring.

"That's freaking convenient," I snarled. I stood up, tossed all my trash on my plate, slammed it in the bin, and walked away with heavy steps. I joined the groups of people walking the aisles where the shops were located.

Ash jogged to catch up with me and asked, "You okay?"

"Yes, and no. I feel okay other than annoyed as all get out. I know she's been through some stuff, but she's not like us, Ash."

"Okay. Tell me what you think and what you feel about her. We will sort it out together."

Ash took my hand and pulled me to a stop close the wall, and then in close to his body. I settled in against him for a moment. I took a long calming breath and said, "I'm better now."

Ash took my hand, and we began to stroll along the mall aisleway. I took another deep breath as his warmth soaked through my skin and helped further calm my emotions.

Then I began to talk about the drive. "She sits up there, silent. But I can feel them talking constantly back and forth. Every now and then you get a Star said this or Star said that, or Star is just weak or anything that has zero substance to it. You ask her a simple question and she doesn't answer it. Oh no, Lark chimes in with Star says."

I leaned heavily on Ash for a second then continued. "I know that doesn't sound all that bad but it's really frustrating. Then there was a time Nora and I were just chatting together in the back, it was nothing exciting or a big deal, but Lark broke in and told us off. Apparently, Star said she was feeling left out. What the hell, Ash? How are we supposed to include her when she won't interact on her own? It is all through a haze of Star says."

"Yeah, sounds like a shit way to spend time trapped in a car."

"You really have no idea," I said.

"Now, think about how she felt to you. What was her energy telling you."

"That's even stranger. A lot of it was as you would expect. Low energy but content. There was one moment though I'm not sure about."

"Okay. I'm listening."

"When Lark was yelling at us for not including Star in our conversation, I felt a zip of joy come from her. Now, don't get me wrong, that spark of joy could have been for many reasons. One being that someone was standing up for her and cared about how she was feeling but it felt funny to me."

"It seems a little off to me too."

"I will say though that part of the issue I have with her, is how we found her and how easy it was to get her out and how easy it was to heal her, and I don't know. Everything feels off when it comes to her. Maybe I am picking at every single thing she does."

"We have had a lot to live through our entire lives. We are allowed to be picky with who we like and who we want to bring into our world. Don't feel bad you aren't trusting at first glance. If it makes you feel any better, Reed and I both feel the same way. Something is just not kosher."

"Okay. Would it be horrible if when we get home, we find her, and if I were to guess, Lark too, their own place to live? I think they are too much for me right now," I said.

"I don't think that's horrible at all. In fact, I love the idea. It will get Lark off our couch, and it will make us all feel a little less anxious. I will go online and see what is available in town. We can couch it as saying Star needs her own space to heal. We all know Lark will go with her so it will be a simple easy way to deal with it."

"Nothing is easy with her and if it is, it's suspect," I said.

On the next leg of the journey Nora and I rode with Reed. I made Ash ride with Lark and Star just to keep an eye on them. He didn't complain too much. Nora and I were happy to feel free to talk and we spent the time hashing out our thoughts on the Star and Lark situation.

"I asked Ash to help find Star her own place to stay," I told them.

"Thank goodness for that," Nora said. "I don't feel like sleeping with one eye open. She is the sort that would knife you in your sleep!"

"Do you really think that?" I asked.

Nora thought about it for a moment then said, "I can't tell. She's such a question. Maybe if she talked it would help. It feels like she is hiding something from us because she refuses to communicate."

"Plus, the whole deal feels hinky," Reed added.

We stopped one more time for dinner, then found a place to stay for the night. We went on the next day the same as the day before. We took turns in the Lark and Star car of misery to keep an eye on them. Reed and Ash both said the same thing, "It's so awkward. Why won't she just talk?"

We finally made it home safe. We were all tired and I don't know about the others, but I was cranky and sick of being in the car. As we were unloading, I was immediately annoyed even more, because Star sat on the step by the door to the house and watched us. She didn't help at all. I sent out a little touch of energy and she was not sick. She was not hurt. She had been eating and sleeping and sitting in the car like the rest of us for two plus days and she couldn't lift a finger to help?

"You're doing it again," Ash said chuckling.

I looked up from the car, I was strongly staring at, so I didn't glare at Star and asked, "What?"

He tilted his head to the grass behind me and low and behold, those damn daisies were there in a little path following me up to the house.

Reed smiled and said, "No hiding your emotions, eh? You have tattle tale flowers to give you away."

"Star says, it's a funny side effect to have just for being pregnant," Lark said chuckling. "She's not wrong either."

I slowly turned and had no issue glaring hard and steady at Lark. "What did you say?"

He frowned. Ash was not frowning. He was scowling and his face was a bit pink in the cheeks. "Did I miss something," Lark asked.

"How would she know?" I asked. The entire driveway and yard where we stood went silent. The birds quieted. The bugs and other insects stopped moving or making any sounds at all. It was like a calm before a giant storm.

I was trying to hold in my gifts, and I was trying to hold onto my temper, but I knew I was losing. The daisies were thick under my feet now and spreading outward toward Lark and Star.

Lark looked around and then landed on Nora and Reed for help. Not sure what he thought they were going to do. He finally stuttered out a reply, "She's one of us. I thought she should know."

I didn't get a chance to react. Ash sprung forward and tackled Lark. Lark may be bigger and look buff and strong, but Ash was furious with good reason.

They fell to the ground in a tangle of thrashing arms and legs, peppered with grunts and heavy breathing. "It was not your secret to tell," Ash ground out at him as he swung a fist and landed it on Lark's face.

I ran forward and called to Reed and said, "Help me."

We both reached into the mix and yanked and pulled them apart. They were panting and red in the face, and they were eye to eye staring daggers at one another.

"Stop it!" I said to them both.

Reed stepped between them and held Ash back with a hand on his chest. He shook his head once and said, "Don't."

Star I noticed had hardly moved a muscle from the step. She did stand up but that was all. I turned back to the men and said, "Ash is right. Lark that was not your secret to tell."

"I don't understand you guys. If we are all part of the same team, why wouldn't you tell her?"

"Because we don't know her. She isn't part of our team yet. She's just some girl with gifts who doesn't interact or talk to any of us but you. We don't trust her."

"That's not fair, Eve," Lark said.

I nodded and said, "Yes, it is. You haven't lived our lives. You haven't lived our terror and torture and fear. You don't get to decide what we do and who we let into our group. We decide. You have no idea what we are up against."

I pointed at Star and said, "She maybe has a small idea of what we face, but even she hasn't lived our life. You didn't just put me and the others in danger. You put a baby in danger. What do you think will happen when they find out I am having a baby, and it could have natural, biological gifts?"

He went silent.

"No. You get to answer me. What do you think will happen?" I demanded.

He shook his head, and said, "I don't know."

I huffed out a laugh, but it was not a joyful one. It was sarcastic and mean and on purpose. "I will tell you then. They will stop at nothing to get to her. They will kill us all and take her and experiment on her for as long as she lives."

The sky darkened and thunder rolled behind me. I stepped closer to Lark and snarled, "She will be in pain and will suffer. That is what will happen, and you just let some stranger, that we found at SaneCorp, know all about us and about the baby. She could have a tracker in her or on her. She could be a spy for all we know and will be contacting them to give them information about us. No. She is not one of us."

"She is," he replied.

I shrugged and said, "How would you know? You don't even know what we are."

"Eve, she has been through a lot too," he said, but I cut him off.

"How would we know. She doesn't talk to us!" I shouted the last bit at him. "She only talks to you, in your head."

"She doesn't want to talk yet," he said.

"So what? Either she starts talking to us and not through you as her personal little telephone, or she gets the hell out of here and away from us. She's free and healed. She's out of the cage and away from SaneCorp. She can leave."

"You would just kick her to the curb and make her leave?" He asked.

"Yeah, I would in a heartbeat," I said. I indicated the others and said, "I think they would too."

The other stayed quiet. Maybe they thought it was a family fight, so they didn't intrude.

"I won't let her go alone. If you make her leave, I will go with her," Lark said softly.

I tried to temper my anger, but I was mad for a good reason and finally I said, "You are a big boy now. You can stay or go. I don't care."

His face fell and I could see the hurt I'd inflicted. I meant what I said though. He was a grown man and could take care of himself. My baby couldn't.

I turned and headed to the house just as it started to rain. My anger had slipped away and in its place was just complete sadness. My brother would choose that girl. I'd lose him all over again. Only this time, I'd remember it.

I didn't want to hear anything else from anyone. I didn't even look behind me to see if a trail of those stupid daisies led the way. I stepped around Star without giving her a second look and went inside, the door slamming shut behind me.

Once in the door, I stopped and took several deep breaths to try to calm down. Outside was one thing with the daisies, but inside was not where any of us wanted them. Once I felt calmer, I stepped into the kitchen and began to make a mental note of things we needed from the store.

It was a menial brainless task, but that was exactly what I needed. About ten or fifteen minutes went by before Ash, Nora and Reed stepped inside and into the kitchen with me. "Sorry for my outburst. I was very angry," I said.

"You had every right to be," Nora said.

"Are they still outside?" I asked.

Nora shook her head and said, "No. Reed found them a little trailer about two miles south. They are going over to give it a look. Lark promised to come over tomorrow alone and talk to you when everyone is calmer."

I nodded my understanding and turned to look out the window.

"So," Ash said. "She?"

I turned and looked at him with what I am sure was a very confused look. "What?"

"You called our nugget she," he said.

I was surprised for a second, but then I reached out to the baby and realized I'd known all along, I'd just been hiding from it. "Yes. Oh my gosh, yes. I just realized it. She's a girl."

Nora not one for physical affection with anyone but Reed actually came and gave me a hug and said, "Congratulations momma."

I was so happy about the baby being a girl, and yet scared at the same time. Having these gifts and powers was hard for us all. Add in being a girl and all that comes with it, and it's harder in some respects. If she was gifted like us, it would be even worse.

"We have to deal with SaneCorp," I said. After a second, I said, "and I think Star."

Ash shook his head and said, "Eve, we don't know the deal with her. We shouldn't just assume she's on the wrong side of things. We don't know what she's been through. We don't know who she is. All we know is she was trapped in a cage, tortured, starving, and alone."

Reed chimed in too and said, "Although you all know how much I hate to agree with the fire man, he's right. We know what we have survived. We know what we had to do in order to survive. We should give her a chance to tell us her story."

Nora pulled a snarly face. One I appreciated as I felt the same. She said, "And how exactly would you like her to tell us her story when she won't talk. I am not going to take the word of Lark with the whole she said thing. She either tells us her side so we can figure out how to help her or she is out. We set her free, she can do whatever she wants from there."

"She doesn't know us either," Reed said. "Why should she trust us?"

"Seriously?" I snapped. "Because we set her free. I healed her. We've gotten her out of SaneCorp and to safety. She either trusts us or she doesn't, and she can head on down the road. I don't care. Yes, that's mean and not usually my standard operating procedure, but I have more to think about than just us. I have a baby to think about. She's coming in like four more months."

"I'm with Eve. We have just a handful of months to deal with SaneCorp. We are further from our goal now than we were a week ago. We can't just trust Star because of how we found her. We are smarter than that," Nora said.

"You all know I lived on a little farm in New Mexico for a long time. I always told you that SaneCorp left me alone as I was easy to be found if I stayed there. What I didn't tell you is that they were always watching. They were always just waiting for the time they were told to grab me. I made a little family on that farm, but not all the people there were family. Some were paid spies made to appear to be my friends."

"I'm sorry, Eve." Ash said.

"I know how that feels too," Reed said.

Nora also gave her two cents. "That's why I didn't trust anyone." Which we all knew was crap as she had Nancy for a while. The woman she worked with at the little diner. She trusted her with her secret and her heart.

None of us called her on the little fib though, as I had a feeling, we all also knew Nancy was one of the very few to get that trust. "It was my own fault," I said. "I could feel something was off with some of them, but I was too young and yes naïve to know any better. It doesn't mean it didn't hurt when the realizations came, and I learned a hard lesson from it too. I may look sweet and giving on the outside, but inside, I'm just as untrusting and selfish as the rest of you."

"Keep telling yourself that, babe," Ash said as he pulled me in for a tight hug. "You are that sweet and giving person. Even if you hate it sometimes. That is why this is hard for you. You just got Lark back and you know, if they are paired like we are, he will go with her without question."

I leaned into him but spoke to the group. "I just got him back. I don't want him to leave, but if she doesn't open up to us, we can't let her stay."

"We all are on the same page with that Eve," Nora said. She stood in the circle of Reed's arms and leaned against him as I did Ash. "We have come a long way from when we first met when we didn't trust anyone or each other. I say we give her a chance, but if she doesn't take it, she has to go. We have too much at stake here."

We all agreed with the plan to talk to Lark in the morning. We would give Star a chance. That was all we could promise. I was exhausted and the day had been really long. "I'm heading to bed."

"I think we all are," Reed said. "I'll lock up."

I turned toward my room but stopped. "You think we're safe here now? If SaneCorp did know we were coming, doesn't that mean they know where we are? That they have been watching us this whole time?"

Nora shrugged just one shoulder and said, "They have always known where we are. It's not new. You know that. You just don't like it."

I sighed. She was right. "Do you think they will come for us?"

"I don't think they are ready for us," Reed said. "Together we are a force. They need to figure out how to deal with us as that force before they can take us."

Ash squeezed me close to his body and said, "Let them come. We will face them if they do. We are okay."

I nodded and said, "Okay. Night then." Ash and I walked into our room and shut the door behind us. I locked it. Just in case.

Chapter Thirteen

"Lark, you have to understand, we don't trust anyone. The fact she won't talk to us, just you, doesn't help," Ash said trying to make him understand.

We were all outside just after noon in the warm heat of the day. I stood so the sun hit my back and warmed me from the outside in. Some would say it was too hot, but I was soaking up the energy the sun was giving me.

"She doesn't trust you guys either. Why should she talk to you? You make her feel like a criminal."

"We make her feel. Are you kidding me?" Nora snapped. She stepped in close to Lark and said, "You don't get to judge us, and she sure as hell doesn't."

The temperature dropped a good ten degrees almost immediately in the area around us all.

I could feel static electricity building in the air around us too. That I think was Lark.

I took a deep loud breath and said, "Okay, guys. We have to come to an agreement here. How to move forward. Lark, there is no halfway with Star. She either has to tell us who she is, how she got mixed up with SaneCorp, and what she plans for her future, or she can't stay. I'm sorry, but that's how it is going to be."

The air warmed as Nora settled. The static sorta blew off. I would guess that was Reed's doing. Everyone took a moment and calmed down.

"I can't make her talk," Lark said running his fingers angrily through his hair. He was obviously still agitated, but more in control. I would guess he had been trying to solve the issue directly with Star too. Apparently, he was not getting anywhere with her either.

Nora turned away from the group and looked out over the back garden. She was a strong force, and her temper could rival us all. The fact she was trying to keep it in check meant all the world to me.

"That's not much to ask for," Reed said. "You know it's not."

"It's her choice what she wants to do. Stay or go. You can't make her talk, and we don't have to allow her to stay," Ash said and shrugged. "She decides your fate. Make sure it's one you want."

"I'll go talk to her," Lark said.

I held in the snort I so wanted to express. "Lark, has she spoken to you out loud at all? Even once?? I mean you said she won't talk to us because she doesn't trust us, but she obviously trusts you. Has she talked to you? Have you heard her voice?"

He shook his head. I felt his discomfort at that revelation.

"Are you sure she can talk?" I asked, hoping maybe she lied as she was afraid of our reaction. Because she hadn't talked out loud to Lark either, that was another big giant red flag on her back waving in the wind.

Lark didn't answer my question. He just opened the door to the car and heavily dropped into the driver's seat. "I'll text you in a bit. Let you all know the plans," he said then closed the door, started up the car, and drove away.

"Ash, you want to go up to the Farmer's Market so I can let Connie know we're back?" I asked.

"Sure," he said. "You guys coming too? Or are you staying here?"

"I'm coming. We need to get some things in town, and I should stop in at the pizza place too. They can get me back on the schedule tomorrow if they want," Nora added.

"Well, hell. I'll do the same. May as well get back to usual. You ready to go right this second or you need a few?" Reed asked.

"Meet you all at the car in five," I said and went inside to get some shoes on and pull my hair up.

The market was hopping, even for a Saturday. There were loads of people around, but that was always good for the vendors. I'd be back at my own spot, on Monday. I stopped at a few of the booths to buy fun unnecessary things like organic vanilla ChapStick and a jar of salsa. Then I got to the bread table and Connie, where I filled up on fresh yeasty bread. My favorite.

"Hey you! I didn't expect you back for another day or so. How was the trip?" She asked.

"It was good," I said. There wasn't much I could tell her so I focused on what I could to fill in the blanks. "I am glad to be out of the car!"

That made her laugh, which was my plan. "I bet! What did you do. Were you able to find anything fun."

"Well, we ate at a lot of greasy road type restaurants and saw a lot of land and little towns. There were no big plans, just to get out and drive really. It was perfect in that regard," I said. Next trip we would have to do something fun in between so when anyone asked, we had stories to tell. All I had was driving, sneaking around in the dark, and breaking into buildings. I couldn't really share that.

"We did more than that," Ash said. "There was one night we went for a walk through a forest. The moon was almost full, and the forest smelled heavily of pine. It was a gorgeous night for a nature walk. Besides, anything I do with you is an adventure." He kissed me on the cheek and winked.

"Aw," Connie cooed. "He's a keeper."

I laughed. "Yeah, he's cute." Then I changed the subject and asked, "How's business been?"

"We are in a busy cycle. It's been like this all week. Lots of people asking where you were. I told them you went on vacation and would be back in a week. You had some veggies ripening and I thought about bringing them in to sell for you, but I didn't. I didn't know if you would be okay with that or not, so I left it alone."

"I hadn't thought about that. I would have been okay with it though for future reference. I hate when produce goes bad. I should have told you to take anything you wanted. I'm sorry. That was wasteful."

"Nah," she said and waved me off. "Next time we will plan it out better."

There were people crowding up around us, so I said, "We'll get out of your way. I'll see you Monday." Then I turned to Ash and said, "Ready."

We wandered a bit more through the rest of the booths and then headed over to the pizza place where we said we'd meet up with the others. While there we had a late lunch.

Honestly, we were really just counting time, waiting for Lark to text us. How long could it take to talk her into telling us what was really going on with her? I mean really.

Apparently, it took all afternoon as the text from Lark didn't come until just before dinner and all it said was, "On our way."

"What's the plan," Ash asked the others.

"I think we should just ask her to tell us her story. The main story being how she got mixed up with SaneCorp," I said.

"What will that really tell us?" Nora asked.

"It will tell us if she hooked up with them voluntarily. If she wanted powers. Why maybe she did it. It will hopefully tell us if she is a good person or not. I'm not sure there are any good answers when it comes to the future, but they could be good answers into who she is," Ash said.

"We didn't get a choice in our lives. We were just created on the whims of our parents and the scientists. Then we had to live with their choices," I said. Then after a moment I added, "I know our powers are cool. I love all I can do and create. I love seeing the power of Nora's ice and Ash's flames. Reed is a force we don't even know what all he can do yet. But…I would give it all up to live a normal life and to not have to look over my shoulder for the rest of my life."

"In a heartbeat, I would too," Nora said. She shrugged one shoulder and then added, "But then I wouldn't have found Reed and you guys."

I looked at Ash and thought about a life without him in it and I felt a painful pang in my chest. I placed my hand on my slowly growing tummy and thought about the loss of the little nugget too, and the pang grew. "Maybe the creation of us and our having to live with the consequences of it, are not all bad," I said and reached for Ash's hand.

He looked down at me and said, "I'd trade almost anything for you."

"Barf," Reed said and pulled a disgusted face.

"So, you don't feel the same way," Nora asked.

"I didn't say that" he said, and his disgusted face turned to one of momentary panic before it settled into his standard stoic unemotional self.

"You implied," Nora pressed.

"No, I implied that their lovely dovey crap was grossing me out," Reed said.

"Would you trade me and you for our freedom," she asked point blankly.

He didn't hesitate for a moment. "No." That was all he said, but that was enough for Nora apparently as she wrapped her arms around his waist and laid her head on his chest in a show of love and contentment.

I heard a car pull into the driveway and turned to see the beat-up piece of junk that Lark was driving. He was alone. That did not bode well for any of us.

He stepped out of the car and straightened up to his full height and walked purposefully over to where we were standing. "Hey," he said.

"Hey," I said back.

"Where's Star?" Nora asked.

"That was the point of the meeting," Ash said.

Reed said nothing, he simply stared at Lark with a heavy frown.

"She's nervous," Lark said.

"So," I replied.

"So, she was wondering if you girls could meet for like coffee, instead of a giant group staring at her like she was a bug."

I turned to the others and took in their expressions and felt for the energy coming off them. "Does she really think we would hurt her? I healed her. Why would I undo all my work?"

"She doesn't think you will hurt her. She just doesn't want a grand production of who she is. She would prefer to do it in smaller setting. That's why I suggested you and Nora."

I turned to Ash and asked without words what he thought about it. Ash understood immediately and said, "Reed and I can drop you ladies off and run a few errands. We can give her this. It's an easy one."

Reed stayed silent for a long moment. I thought he was going to say he didn't like it, but instead he surprised me and said, "Don't look at me, Nora can make her own decisions."

"We know she can. That's not what we are asking," I said. "I want to know what you think about the situation."

"I don't like it," he said. "The whole thing feels off."

I agreed with him. Something did feel weird. The whole situation was weird. We needed to figure out why though. "What time?"

"How about in half an hour? You can meet at the Pour and Sip place over on Main," Lark said.

"Are you coming or just dropping her off too?" I asked.

"I said I'd give her some privacy to talk with you and Nora, so I will be dropping off too.

~ * ~

Nora and I arrived at the Pour and Sip as requested and right on time. It was a quaint little coffee shop decorated in yellows and browns with little coffee beans painted on the walls. There were photographs of actual beans framed here and there, which I thought was too cute. It was a small shop. It had the bar where they made the coffee and the little case that usually held some type of pastries and sugary options to choose from to go with your coffee. Then there were about 8 tables where customers could sit and enjoy.

We went up to the bar and placed our orders before going to find a place to sit that was a little private at least. We chose a seat near the back. It was in a corner that had windows along the side and the back so we could see the door and would be blanketed in sunshine as well. It felt like a good choice.

I sipped on my decaffeinated hot mocha-chino while I jealously looked at Nora's full caffeine laced caramel latte. I knew she should probably not be drinking that, but she didn't. Not yet. I figured it would be soon though. I wondered how far apart our pregnancies were. A few months? Couldn't be much more. She had to be about two by now. I was about five months gone.

As I sat there and dreamed about our children growing up together and having a best friend from almost day one, I felt a little fluttering in my stomach. Nothing big or defined. Like little wings dancing about. "Oh!" I said and placed my hand where the feeling was.

"What's wrong?" Nora asked, her eyes wide and concerned.

I felt my eyes burn and start to tear up. "Nothing. Nothing is wrong," I said.

She reached for her phone and started to type, "Then why are you crying. I'm calling Reed."

"No, honestly. Nora, I just felt the baby move," I said with a watery smile.

"Oh," she said and set her phone back down. "Yeah, that's definitely worth a tear or two."

"You'd think because I can reach out to her with my mind that feeling her move wouldn't be so exciting and wonderful, but it is. It tells me she is growing just like she is supposed to. She is doing all the things a normal baby would do. It makes me happy, scared, and elated all at once."

"I can only imagine, Eve." Nora glanced toward the door and then said in a quiet voice, "Sop it up though, cause here she comes."

I shook my head and chuckled at Nora. She had such a way with words. I smiled at Star and gave a wave. She nodded at me and stepped to the counter to place her order.

Lark and Star must have gone shopping, as Star was outfitted in slim light blue jeans, and a flowy yellow tank top. Her hair was styled in shiny soft waves of golden brown that danced around her waist when she walked.

A small knot formed in my gut as I realized Star placed an order. Easily. No hesitation. She walked up and asked for a large chai latte. Her voice was sweet and had a musicality in its cadence, which rang softly through the shop.

"Nora," I said. I didn't have to say anything else.

"Yeah, me too," she replied.

After Star paid and made her way to our table, I tried to send her another welcoming smile, but I wasn't sure I'd pulled it off as she didn't smile back. She sat down in the chair that put her back to the door.

That was a move none of us would have made. That showed she was not afraid. Or hadn't learned to be afraid. We'd see which one that was. Since you can't watch your own back, we tended to try and place ourselves in a space where our back was covered. Star didn't seem to care that she couldn't see the door and who or what was coming in behind her.

"So, have you figured it all out yet?" Star said clearly and with a bit of sad inflection.

I looked at Nora for confirmation who gave a very slight shake of her head and then I said, "No. I'm not sure we have."

Star shrugged and said, "Do you know that although Lark doesn't have your gifts, and is nowhere near as strong in a gift that the rest of us are, he does have a power all of his own?"

I shook my head in answer and said again, "Yes. He mentioned that."

Star smiled. It was one of pride. I wondered if it was pride, from her knowing something we didn't think she should know, or was it pride in Lark?

"He is an honest to God lie detector. All he has to do is hear your voice and he will know, just know, whether or not you are telling the truth or if you are lying. He can even tell if you are hiding something and not telling the full truth."

"That's why you won't talk," Nora said.

It all just hit me like a ton of bricks. I'd known there had to be a real reason she would not use her voice. I knew it, but I let my sympathy and desire for Lark to be happy to cloud my instincts. I knew better than that. We all did.

"How did you know that about him?" I asked.

She looked at Nora and me, lowered her voice a bit and said, "I could read his mind the moment he walked in the door. He has zero barriers in there."

"He's not needed them," I snapped.

"I'm not insulting him," she said with a bit of hurt in her tone. She was not making any sense.

"Are you even really paired with him or is that all lie too?" I asked.

"No, that's true. I swear I would never lie about that," Star said.

I didn't want to believe her, as she was one big lie all wrapped up in a pretty bow, but I did. Her eyes were where you could see inside of her. Her eyes didn't lie.

"The moment I reached out to his mind, something opened in me and connected with him. I'd never felt anything like it before in my whole life. He is what I have been searching for. He is mine and I will do anything to keep him."

"He's not a puppy!" Nora snapped. "You don't get to keep him or possess him. That's not how it works."

Star looked down for a moment then lifted angry eyes at both Nora and me. "Are you really so different? What would you do to keep your man?"

My mind shouted at me that yes, I would do anything for Ash. But would I? Would I harm others? Would I turn all I was into evil? I don't know. I didn't think so or maybe I hoped I wouldn't.

"I would do just about anything for Reed," Nora said. "I don't know that I would harm others for him though. He fell in love with me because I am who I am, and my ethics and morals are part of that. I don't think he would feel the same about me if I didn't have those foundations."

"Same," I said. "Part of what Ash loves about me is the person inside where no one can see. The part that makes me, me. You are not giving Lark that person. You are holding the real you back. Are you afraid he won't like you if he knows who you really are?"

It sounded mean when I said it out loud, but it was something I really wanted to know.

Star looked down at her folded hands for a long few minutes. They were sitting on the table before her. It was an awkward time.

I finally broke the silence and asked, "How did you get involved with SaneCorp? Let's start there."

"I don't know that you would understand. You guys have it all. Have always had your powers and gifts. I didn't. I came from nothing. We were poor and everyone always whispered about us being trash. I never had any friends. My parents worked all the time, so I was alone all the time. I tried to make friends, but I was made fun of for my clothes. I was clean but they talked about me like I was dirty and smelled. I didn't! I knew one day I would show them, all of them, that I was more than just a poor kid from the trailer park. I was more. I am more."

"Why would you think we had it any better?" Nora asked. "You know nothing about us either. Not where we come from. Not what we've survived. You know our names and that's it. You are part of your own problem."

"Maybe," Star said. "But I am going to be something, something phenomenal. I will show them all."

She stopped and took a drink from her cup then continued. "They sought me out. SaneCorp did. I was working in a little restaurant, and they sat at my table and asked me about myself, did I have family, and friends. That sort of thing."

Spark

I knew they were asking because they didn't want anyone to look for her if she didn't come home one night. They weren't interested in her, Star. They were invested in what defenses she would have against them.

"They asked me if I would be interested in being a part of their study on ESP. That sounded really cool, and I asked what type of study and asked if I would get paid."

"So, you were okay being a scientific guinea pig, as long as they paid you?" Nora snarked.

"They paid me a lot of money to be their guinea pig," she said and held out her hands to us. "And I have these powers now. Even better they paired me with Lark, so I won't be alone anymore. I have all I ever wanted. Someone to love and love me back and power I control and contain within me. It is worth all I had and have to do to get here."

"What else do you have to do?" I asked, suddenly a little apprehensive. Actually, that's not even accurate. Dread is what I was feeling as I began to piece together what she was doing.

"The experiment was more than I could have asked for. I can read minds. I can communicate with my mind. I can make wind. I am going to be someone now. I am going to be rich and powerful, and no one can stop me."

Nora laughed. It was a mean laugh and at another time I would have tried to temper the mean with my calm, but not this time. I let her be. I felt what she was feeling and knew before she said it what she was going to say.

Nora leaned forward to Star and said, "You are a dumb ass."

Okay that I didn't expect. The next part, yes.

"SaneCorp gave you that power. They can take it away too. You are an idiot if you think otherwise. The moment they are done using you, they will hunt you down and bring you back in. They will make you into whatever they want you to be for them."

"That's not true," Star said.

Nora shook her head and cut her off. "Why do you think we live like we do? Why do you think we are trying to take them down? They will never stop hunting us or you. Ever."

Star looked from Nora to me. I slowly nodded my head in agreement.

"No. That can't be true," she said.

160

"Don't be naive. You know it is," Nora said.

"Look what they did just to make it possible for you to join us. They obviously beat you and starved you, all on the chance we might find you and then decide to help you. You accepted that treatment and prison. What will you accept next time? Will you kill for them?"

"No. You are twisting things around. They are just trying to stop you guys from destroying everything. You…you are the bad guys. Not them." She said it as a statement, but it also sounded like a desperate question.

"You believe what you want. But remember this. If you hurt Eve, Lark will never forgive you. Pairing or not, he will never forgive you. That's the hard and honest truth. Decide which side you are on," Nora said.

I took hold of her very small and cold hand and said, "You can read his mind, right? What do you see when you look inside his heart? Can you read his feelings and emotions? If you haven't, you should. That type of energy doesn't lie. If you like him and are paired with him as you say, you better be sure on what you're doing."

She was silent for a long moment. You could see she was thinking and trying to figure things out. I and Nora, both let her. She would have to decide who was evil on her own. After a few minutes I looked at the time on my phone and said, "We should get home."

That spurned Star into action. She grabbed hold of both our hands and all but shouted, "We have to get out of here. Come on."

I didn't ask questions. That is one thing I have learned, when people sound distressed, just do as they say when you can. In this instance, I felt her sudden fear in the air as it bounced off her skin. I jumped up and moved toward the front door.

I bumped into the back of Star as she came to a sudden stop. "What?" I asked and peered around her to see two men enter the shop.

"SaneCorp," Nora whispered. "Star, what have you done?"

Chapter Fourteen

The men didn't need to introduce themselves as SaneCorp men. We could all just tell. There was no guess work this time. They wore dark suits, and had big, huge beefy builds that screamed steroids. Their hair was short to the scalp or just bald. One big giveaway was that all the SaneCorp men I'd dealt with always had these straight dead expressions. There was no mistaking them once they were right in front of you. Add in the fact I felt their energy and recoiled from the hate within it.

"I thought I was doing the right thing. I thought you were the bad guys. I don't know if I am right or not, but this feels wrong." She dragged us around in a circle and headed back in the direction we'd come, toward the back of the place. "We have to get out of here."

"There isn't a back exit," Nora said as she jerked her hand free from Star and turned to face the threat head on.

I stood strong next to her, shoulder to shoulder, and carefully whispered, "Don't let them win. They can't take you. But if they do, if they take us, do not let them take your blood."

She jerked around to face me. Her expression one of confusion, "Why? They already have buckets of it."

I reached out with a very soft touch with my energy to make sure, one more time, just to be absolutely certain, and found what I was looking for. A very faint, but also strong, heartbeat. Life, growing inside Nora, quietly, and secretly.

I shook my head. "It's different now. I'm sorry. I wanted you to have time to figure it out on your own, but there isn't time for that. You're pregnant."

"The hell I am!" She shouted.

Had it been any other time I would have laughed. This time all I could do was nod. "Yes, you are."

She stared at me with a mixture of emotions bright on her face. Fear, awe, surprise, even a bit of happiness. Then she nodded once at me, I assumed to mean she decided to believe me. Maybe she'd already had suspicions. Maybe she just trusted me. Either way, she accepted it.

"They aren't taking us," she said and widened her stance with her arms held next to her body with her hands wide open. She took long deep breaths. I knew this was to gather as much moisture from the air as possible. She was ready to fight.

I turned to Star and said, "Choose, Star."

She was shaking her head. I yelled at her now, "It's now or never!"

The temperature in the shop dropped a good twenty degrees in moments and continued to fall rapidly. The shop was small and not very busy, but we were not alone in it. There were several people in there with us. Two people behind the counter and a few customers. "You all should leave," I said. "I'm sorry, but it's about to get loud and dangerous in here."

The edges of all the windows began to frost over and little flakes of snow began to slowly fall around us. "Hang on Nora," I said gently wanting to give the people inside a chance to get out. The two behind the counter rushed around the side and headed to the door with the others.

"There isn't time to hang on," she said.

A wind began to whirl around us, and Star stepped up next to me on the other side from Nora. "Okay. I'm trusting you guys."

I turned to her and asked, "Can you communicate with Lark from this far away? Or do you need to be close to him?"

She didn't take her eyes off the two guys at the door blocking our escape. "I don't know. I've never tried."

"Try now!" Nora snapped. She was getting angry. Which for us was good generally but it made it hard to reason with her too.

"Can you try?" I asked Star with a more moderate tone than Nora had used. If Star was able to help us, we needed her too. I didn't want her to get a burr up her behind and change sides again.

"Yes," she answered. Then said, "They are about to rush us."

I widened my stance like Nora and began to call to the earth and all the life inside it and around it. The ground underneath our feet began to rumble as I pulled life from it. The tiles at the door just behind the two men broke away. A long dark green vine began to slither its way out from the ground and grow in thickness and length. If they made a move, I would use it to grab them back and maybe toss them away.

The guy on my right turned to his buddy and smiled. He then took out a gun and aimed it at Nora. She was poised to let her ice go and take them out.

The wind around us was growing in strength. It was blowing my hair around my head and into my face.

"Can you read their minds," I asked Star.

Before she could answer me, the gun moved from Nora's direction to mine, and without a moment's hesitation he shot.

I felt a small sting of pain on my neck. I reached up to feel it, more out of instinct than thought. I felt something small and hard stuck to me. I grabbed it, pulled it away with a tearing pain, to see what it was. "Oh my, God, Nora."

She turned and saw what I held in my palm, and it was almost like the last piece of a puzzle she needed. She let her ice loose. It shot out from her hands toward the men. The wind around us where before it had felt uncontrolled and wild, found a pointed direction and it pushed the ice harder and faster as it flowed.

It hit the men with a force they were not prepared for, and they fell back a few steps. They froze in place quickly, their bodies covered and cemented within a wall of ice. The vines I had prepared quickly wrapped around them, knotted and circled and encased them as tightly as the ice had. They weren't going anywhere. In fact, they were never going anywhere again. Frozen solid as they were within the pod, there was zero life energy coming from them.

"Are they dead," Star asked quietly.

"Yep," Nora said as she grabbed me and made me sit on the floor. "Are you alright?"

"My vision is getting hazed around the edges and I feel my muscles weakening, but otherwise I'm okay," I said. "Star, were you able to connect with Lark? Are the guys coming?"

"Yes." Then, "You killed them."

Nora shook her head and said, "No. We killed them. You get as much credit as us."

"I've...never done that before."

"We don't do it often," I snapped, feeling sick and woozy. My head felt too heavy on my neck, and it wobbled about out of my control. As it fell backward, I caught a movement behind us. I tried to control my muscles enough to make my eyes focus in on that area, but my eyes were darkening further and further as every second went by. "Nora."

A whole fleet of men suddenly poured into the shop. They raised their guns without any warning or conflict and shot at us with the little tubes filled with chemicals, that I had no idea what they were, other than they were about to knock me out.

The group was focused in on Nora, but the wind picked up fast, thanks to Star and helped to deflect them away from all of us. Nora stood and turned and faced them head on.

I was fading away and of almost no use by this time. All I could do was lay on the ground. I could hardly move at all. My body felt like it was freezing up from the inside out.

Nora faced off against a group of at least seven men. She threw ice shards at them and took several of the front runners out fast. Star stepped in front of me, next to Nora, and together they fought to hold them off. Someone grabbed my shoulders from behind and began to drag me away.

Star turned toward me. Maybe I'd made a noise. Maybe she sensed the movement. Either way, she turned and screamed, "No!"

I could do nothing but allow the man to drag me off. I couldn't even speak. All I could do was scream inside my head. Fear was coursing through me. Anger was not far behind. Anguish for my child followed.

Nora turned and locked eyes with me. She had one arm facing the group of men and turned the other toward me and the one taking me. If she blasted my way, she'd hit me. We saw the issue and I knew there was nothing she could do. "Eve!" She shouted. Anguish in her voice as it was in my head.

"What do I do!" Star screamed over the noise of the ice, the men, and wind.

Nora looked from me to the front of the shop and all around the building looking for a way to escape and there as none. Not for me anyway. "I don't know."

I saw her jerk back as one of the darts hit home. How many minutes did she have? She should run. I needed her to run. I couldn't tell her that. I tried to form the words, but nothing happened. I don't even know if she would leave me, to save herself anyway, but I was a lost cause at that point. She could get out.

My vision held only small pinpoints of light by then. I was almost gone. I felt myself being lifted and carried like a child. "It will be okay, little one," the man said. Funny thing was, I could tell he really believed it. He was a fool then. Nothing would be alright.

With the last of my vision, I saw Nora fall to the ground and Star screaming "No, this is not what was supposed to happen. You just wanted Eve!"

The men fanned inside easily as Nora was no longer using her ice and the wind had died as Star had given up. One guy picked up Nora and tossed her, not gently over his shoulder. Star tried to hit him and shove at him. She then tried to drag Nora from him.

He just kicked out at her as if she were only an annoying bug. Not worth any of his time or energy. His foot slammed into her stomach. The force of it threw her away from him and to the ground where she landed and lay unmoving.

I'd like to tell you the boys came in with a battle cry full of death and fire, and they saved Nora and me. I can't though. This is not a fairy tale with a happy ending. This, however, is also not the end. It is just a blip in our story. Nora and I were taken. That could not be stopped as SaneCorp had been smart. They got Star to separate us from the others. Knowing we were all stronger together, and the more we were separated, the more chance they had at getting to me, to us.

We had not expected them to come for us in broad daylight. That was our mistake. They had not expected Star to turn on them and stand to fight with us. That was their mistake. Didn't matter as in the end, they hauled Nora and I off all the same.

My last sight, before the darkness took over me, was of the ceiling of the coffee shop. It had white fancy tiles with raised tulips on them. They were faded to a dusty white but still beautiful with their art. I could hear the whomp whomp of a helicopter in the distance along with sirens and horns. Help was on the way, but it would come too late. Finally, the darkness closed in. I saw and heard nothing else.

To be continued…

Also by the Author
at
Rogue Pheonix Press

Cold
Elements Book 1

Four extraordinary teens, each with a corrupted gift from one of the four elements: Water, Earth, Wind, and Fire, come together to face a common threat. Their creators, scientists of a genetic engineering company, have been hunting for them since they were children. Each alone and on the run for years, they inexplicably find one another and decide not to hide any longer. Before they can face their creators, they have to learn to trust one another as well as who they are and what they can do. *Cold* is Nora's story. Water is destructive all by itself but turn water to ice and it can become even more deadly, especially in the hands of an angry young woman out to right a wrong.

Shadow Dancer
Shadow Dancer Book 1

Sunny has a gift that she has no idea how to use, until she meets Leif, a boy from the kingdom of Acadia, on the other side of the shadows.

Leif teaches Sunny about Shadow Walkers and how to use her newfound gifts. As they grow closer and their gifts grow stronger, a threat arrives. The Shadow Guard has been sent to bring Sunny back to Acadia, to determine if she is a threat to the king as the rightful ruler of Acadia.

As Leif and Sunny prepare to defend themselves, Sunny finds that Leif has also been sent to bring Sunny back to the kingdom but for very different reasons. As a battle for possession of Sunny wages, she is struggling to come to terms with her feelings of inadequacy regarding controlling her gifts as well as the hurt regarding the lies and deceit of everyone around her.

www.ingramcontent.com/pod-product-compliance
Lightning Source LLC
Chambersburg PA
CBHW051959220626

47052CB00004B/1017